Nath
BUTTFACE

NIGEL SMITH has been a journalist, busker, TV
comedy producer and script writer, winning
an award for his BBC 4 radio comedy, *Vent*.
More importantly, he has been – and still is – an
embarrassing dad. Much like Nathalia Buttface,
his three children are continually mortified by
his ill-advised shorts, comedic hats,
low-quality jokes, poorly chosen motor vehicles,
unique sense of direction and unfortunate
ukulele playing. Unlike his hero, Ivor Bumolé,
he doesn't write Christmas cracker
jokes for a living. Yet. This is Nigel's second
book about Nathalia Buttface

Also by the author:

Check out these great reviews from Lovereading4kids:

"The plot was hilarious and the ending was brilliant and unexpected." *Eloise Mae, age 11*

"I couldn't stop laughing." *Sam, age 10*

"This book made me laugh out loud many times and I didn't want it to end." *Lily, age 9*

"One of the funniest books I've read… Seriously hilarious!" *Abigail, age 11*

"I rate this book five stars because it is so funny and really cool." *Jenny, age 8*

"This book is hilarious, amazing and gives me an embarrassing feeling on behalf of Nathalia!" *Elspeth, age 9*

"Nathalia Bumolé is one of the unluckiest kids ever, and most of it is her dad's fault!" *Elise Marie, age 9 ½*

"Makes me glad my dad is nothing like this dad, although he is still very embarrassing." *Emma, age 7*

Nathalia BUTTFACE

and the MOST Epically ~~Embarrassing~~ trip EVER

BY **Nigel Smith**

Illustrated by
Sarah Horne

HarperCollins *Children's Books*

First published in Great Britain by HarperCollins *Children's Books* 2015
HarperCollins *Children's Books* is a division of HarperCollins*Publishers* Ltd,
HarperCollins Publishers,
1 London Bridge Street,
London SE1 9GF

The HarperCollins *Children's Books* website address is
www.harpercollins.co.uk

3

Nathalia Buttface and the Most Epically Embarrassing Trip Ever
Text copyright © Nigel Smith 2015
Illustrations © Sarah Horne 2015

Nigel Smith and Sarah Horne assert the moral right to be identified as
the author and illustrator of this work.

ISBN 978-0-00-754523-0

Printed and bound in England by
Clays Ltd, St Ives plc

To Michèle. Because mums who live with embarrassing dads suffer just as much.

CHAPTER ONE

· · · ·

"I'M NOT GOING ON HOLIDAY TO FRANCE, DAD," SAID Nathalia Bumolé, crossly. "It's rubbish."

The Most Embarrassing Dad in the World paused. He hadn't expected this reaction. In fact, he had come home from the pub with his Great French Holiday Idea feeling really pleased with himself.

Dad *liked* France. He liked the weather and the food and the wine and talking to local people.

"You wear STUPID shorts, your bald spot goes pink and peely, you drink red wine every day and get silly and even more embarrassing than usual and your teeth look like a vampire's," Nat went on, not pausing for breath, "and THE VERY WORST thing is, you talk in a funny accent."

"It's called speaking French."

"It is *not*, Dad, it's called 'speaking English in a silly voice'. You don't even bother to change the words. You are literally supposed to change the words to *actual* French ones. I know that and I'm eleven. BUT I didn't know it at my primary school, did I? In my first French lesson."

Dad put the kettle on. He knew what was coming; he'd heard this story about Nat's first French lesson *a lot*. He looked around the kitchen for support from Mum but she was in the living room. She was pretending to do emails, but she was really playing a game on her phone and having a quiet giggle at Dad being in trouble again.

"Cos of you, when Madame Hérisson asked us who could speak any French, I put my hand up."

"Biscuit?" said Dad, still trying to avoid the story. "There might be one left as your nan's not been here for a couple of days."

But Nat wasn't going to let him escape. She was an angry blur of stick arms and legs and flying blonde hair. Dad was already regretting getting her out of bed to tell her about the Great French Holiday Idea.

Nat advanced on her father. "I put my hand up and said 'Yes, I know French,' and Madame Hérisson said 'Wonderful, come up and tell the class what you had for breakfast, in French.'"

"No custard creams," said Dad, popping the lid of the biscuit tin back on. "I could do you a cheese toastie though?"

But Nat was too busy remembering that horribly embarrassing lesson.

"'Ello my leetle class mateys," Nat had said, confidently, "for brek-farst, I 'ad a sliss of tost." She waited for applause.

"Very amusing," said Madame Hérisson coldly. She didn't look amused. Nat's classmates giggled.

"Zere is nuffink zat iss fuh-nee about a sliss of

tost," Nat continued, still speaking what she now called 'Dad French'.

"Do it properly or sit down," snapped Madame Hérisson, marking Nat out for special attention that year.

Nat pressed on. Perhaps her accent wasn't big enough. She tried Dad French again. "I 'ad ze sliss off tost, and I 'ad a leetle beet of butt-urgh wheech I spred weeeth a ker-nurf." The giggling got louder.

"A ker-nurf?" said Madame Hérisson. "A KER-NURF? What are you talking about, girl?"

"Like a ker-nurf and furk," said Nat. By now the class was in uproar.

"Class clown, are you?" said Madame Hérisson. "Detention."

Dad was *always* embarrassing her. He could even do it when he WASN'T THERE. Of course, it was way worse when he was there. Which was why she had tried so very hard to stop him interfering at her new school.

Epic fail.

It had started on day *one*. Nat's form teacher, Miss Hunny, was an old friend of Dad's (aaarrggh!) and had encouraged Dad to 'join in' at school events (double aaarrggh!).

Dad had very much joined in.

He organised a school trip and lost a pupil AND a teacher.

He put on a quiz night that ended in a riot.

And he was DJ at the end-of-term school disco and accidentally projected Nat's NAKED BABY PHOTOS six metres high in the school hall!

But at least the summer holidays were about to start. After tomorrow, her classmates would have eight weeks to forget about all the disasters Dad had caused. And with a bit of luck they might even forget her horrible surname too.

Even THAT was Dad's fault. Not just because it was *his stupid name*, but because he had managed to reveal it live on air on the breakfast radio show that EVERYONE at Nat's school listened to.

And it didn't matter how many times she

explained 'Bumolé' was pronounced *Bew-mow-lay*. She was still going to be Bum Hole for the rest of her school life, unless everyone developed a very short memory over the summer holidays.

Even her best friend, Darius Bagley, called her Buttface.

Dad was talking again now, doing his gentle voice that drove her nuts.

"Yes yes yes. But let me tell you about my Great French Holiday Idea. It's just brilliant. And the best of it is – it's *free*."

Dad liked free. Dad liked free a bit too much, if you asked Nat. Mum said that in life you get what you pay for. Which is why when Mum went food shopping they got pies with super fluffy crusts full of chunks of tender chicken and veg enfolded in a lovely tasty sauce, perhaps with some rustic hand-cut golden chips.

When *Dad* went food shopping they got a brown pie in a tin.

With a big yellow sticker on it saying: 'Final reduction – eat today if you know what's good for you. May cause swelling and rash if rubbed on skin.'

Mum walked into the kitchen, not smiling any more. Nat *started* smiling. Mum had heard the word 'free' too, and she didn't like the sound of it either.

"What do you mean, Ivor, when you say 'free'?" she purred dangerously.

"I met Posh Barry down the Red Lion tonight," Dad began. Both Nat and Mum groaned. They didn't like Posh Barry very much. To be fair, Nat didn't like any of Dad's friends very much. Because they were all idiots. And when Dad was with them, he became more of an idiot too.

"Posh Barry isn't even posh," said Nat. "He's just one of your stupid old friends from school. He sells scrap. He's always got bits of wire in his hair and he smells like a tin can, so I don't know why you all call him Posh Barry."

"His wife's worse," said Mum, joining in. "'Even Posher Linda' used to be a hairdresser in the high street. She met Barry when he asked her to get the bits of scrap out of his hair. He said it would save him money at the hairdresser's if she married him, so she did. Now she doesn't work and spends most of her time back at her old salon getting her own hair done."

But the absolute *worst* thing about Posh Barry and Even Posher Linda was their ghastly daughter, Mimsy. Mimsy was the year above Nat at school. She was spoilt rotten. She was also very popular, mainly because she gave people gifts all the time. It was only stuff she didn't want any more (or already had a dozen of) but it guaranteed she had loads of friends.

Worse, she had a stupid blog that EVERYONE at school read where she posted about ponies and iPhones and sparkly new trainers and lots of other things that Nat had to pretend she didn't want and wasn't massively jealous of.

Whenever Nat was forced to hang out with Mimsy, Mimsy would always make fun of Nat's clothes, and her rubbish old phone, and, obvs – her embarrassing dad. Which Nat really hated because

SHE was the only person who was allowed to do that. Mimsy liked to put embarrassing photos of Nat's dad on her blog – which, let's be frank, were not hard to find – so everyone at school could have another good laugh at Nat .

"There's no way I'm going to spend my summer holidays hanging out with Mi—"

"Wait! You don't have to. They're not going to be there. Posh Barry has said we can stay in his lovely new house in France this summer – for free! How about that?"

Nat and Mum eyed Dad suspiciously.

"It's a lovely old farmhouse right down in the south, near the sea, with a pool, surrounded by woods, and it's all ours."

"Honestly?" said Mum cautiously.

"Honest!" said Dad. "They said they wouldn't DARE come over till we've finished anyway."

A small warning bell went *clang* in the back of Nat's head. She ignored it, which, she soon realised, was daft.

"In that case, it sounds nice," said mum warily.

"I suppose I should say well done."

"Thought you'd like it," said Dad, giving her a hug.

Eww, Nat cringed. *Parents hugging...*

"Why won't they be there?" said Nat. She knew her dad and his Great Ideas, and had a horrible feeling that there was more to this story than met the eye.

Dad suddenly looked a bit shifty. She'd got him. "Ah well, there is one *tiny* little catch," said Dad. "But it's so small it's hardly worth mentioning..."

Just mention it, Baldy, thought Nat.

"It might need a *tiny* bit of work."

CHAPTER TWO

• • • •

IT NEEDED MORE THAN A TINY BIT. AFTER TWO PINTS of Goblin's Knob ale down the pub, Dad had agreed to: patch the roof, fix the floorboards, mend the hot water boiler, repaint downstairs, re-wallpaper *up*stairs, repair the windows, mow the lawn, and put in a cat flap. After a couple *more* pints he had volunteered to tarmac the drive, plant some trees and get rid of the ghost.

Posh Barry wasn't *absolutely* sure there was a ghost, but his wife Even Posher Linda had 'sensed' something the first night they had stayed there and wasn't going to set foot in the place again until it was got rid of. That was a while ago now, and since then the little French farmhouse had been left to rot.

"A ghost," Nat told Darius the next day at school. "We've got to stay in an old, damp, smelly falling-down house with a ghost. And ghosts don't exist so it'll probably be an axe murderer, hiding out."

"A ghost would be the best pet," said Darius, whose own pet collection consisted of a one-legged frog called Hoppy, a dead slug and a jar of flies. "I could train it to haunt Miss Hunny."

Nat had just moved to the area and so had only been at her new school for the summer term, but Darius Bagley had quickly become her best friend. This was despite him being the naughtiest boy in the school/town/country/world. No one *quite* knew how this had happened, least of all Nat.

But Nat, being fiercely loyal, argued that Darius wasn't so much naughty as just MISUNDER-STOOD. She was also one of the very few people to realise he was both super-bright *and* super-funny, though she did have to admit he was also super-embarrassing (but still not as bad as Dad).

The hot afternoon was dragging on and Nat shifted uncomfortably at her desk. "It's just this woman Linda. She's soft in the head. Dad says when she was a little girl she was scared by a lady with a scarf at Blackpool pleasure beach and since then she's been very sensitive to reverberations."

Nat frowned as she tried to get the story right. "I *think* it was a lady with a scarf. It might have been a donkey with a straw hat; I wasn't really listening. Anyway, it doesn't matter, point is she's bonkers and there's probably no ghost."

Nat was being quite loud but their teacher, Miss Hunny, didn't tell them off for chatting because *everyone* was chatting. It was nearly the end of term and it was too hot even with all the windows open, and Miss Hunny was flicking through the pages of *Last-minute Budget Breaks Magazine*. Rather than getting on with her marking, she was trying to work out how long she could afford to stay in a lovely beach house on a Greek island. On her wages it was about an hour and a half. She slammed the magazine shut sharply.

"I suppose we should get back to our book," sighed Miss Hunny. The class groaned. "Oh don't be like that," she said. "It's a classic."

That made it worse.

Nat knew there were two sorts of classics: old classics and new classics. They were both terrible, especially when the sun was shining outside.

OLD CLASSICS are written by someone who is dead. Women in these books wear bonnets and faint. They are called Mistress Bindweed. Men are rich and rude and have a secret. They are called Captain Stain.

Popular words in old classics include: *periwig*, *effervescent* and *rapscallion*.

NEW CLASSICS are written by intense people about things that REALLY MATTER, OK? And no one faints.

Popular words in new classics include: *innit*, *aggro*, *issues*, *empowered* and *minging*.

No one in the class was keen to get back to Edna O'Dreary's award-winning novel, *My Life, Your Fault*, so a cheer went up when Nat's dreamy friend Penny Posnitch shouted out: "What are you doing in the holidays, Miss?"

It was the old 'ask the teacher about themselves' tactic. Now THAT's a classic.

Miss Hunny was glad to take the bait. She'd had quite enough of Edna O'Dreary too.

"I was invited on a cruise with some friends," she said, "where I could have watched palm trees and golden beaches slip by as I lazed around the ship's pool." Miss Hunny had a faraway look in her eyes. Then she frowned. "But I can only afford a return ticket on the Mersey Ferry."

The class laughed and Miss Hunny muttered something rude under her breath.

Nat hadn't been invited on holiday with any friends that summer, or even round to anyone's house. She had a horrible suspicion part of the problem was the creature sitting next to her, picking his nose and eating the crispy bits.

"What are *you* doing this summer?" Nat asked Darius. "Mutating into a human?"

"I'm going to Norway with My Filthy Granny," he said offhand. Nat was puzzled; she didn't know he had a granny. In fact, she had a theory that Darius was created in a laboratory somewhere.

At home time she found Darius trudging along with her to the school gates. Dad was parked round the corner in his terrible old van, the Atomic Dustbin, because she'd forbidden him to bring it anywhere in sight of the school. Ever since it had exploded in the school car park.

"Give us a lift?" asked Darius. "Oswald can't fetch me, he's in a meeting."

A meeting? thought Nat. *Oswald?*

Darius didn't have any parents; Nat had never asked why, and Darius never wanted to talk about it. Oswald Bagley was Darius's terrifying older brother, who was looking after him. The way wolves sometimes look after man-cubs lost in the forest. Only Oswald was hairier, with more teeth and fleas. He certainly wasn't the kind of person to have a meeting. No one wanted to *meet* him, for a start.

They were just about to leave the school gates when Nat heard a sniggering sort of voice behind her.

"So, I hear you're going to stay in our house in France over the summer?" said Mimsy with a showy-off flick of her hair. "You do *know* it's a wreck right now, don't you? Good luck to you and your TOTAL FAIL of a dad fixing *that* up… It'll probably look even worse by the time he's done with it."

Then Mimsy walked off laughing with her friends and Nat heard the words she'd been dreading: "Don't worry, I'll be blogging *all about it* when I get there. I've got a lush new camera. Wait for the pictures."

"Thanks for sticking up for me, chimpy," Nat said to Darius as he rejoined her.

Darius was staring hard at Mimsy. "Do you fancy her or something?" said Nat crossly.

"Wait," he said mysteriously. "Three… two… one…"

Just then Mimsy shrieked as a huge hole opened up at the bottom of her bulging schoolbag and all the contents spilled out on the floor. Everyone laughed as she scrabbled to pick them up.

For a second Nat thought maybe her suspicions had been right all along and Darius actually WAS the devil, but then she saw him folding up his little pocket knife.

And she remembered why they were friends.

Dad smiled when he saw Darius at the school gates, and the Dog leaped out of the van, scattering pans and boxes and all the other usual van rubbish out on to the pavement as he went. The Dog loved licking Darius as he was the stickiest and therefore the tastiest child he'd ever licked. Nat liked it when Darius got licked by the Dog; at least that got him clean.

Dad chatted about his Great French Holiday Idea all the way to Darius's house. All Darius wanted to know about was the ghost. "Is it a strangling ghost, a restless spirit that throws things about, or a blood-sucking phantom?" he asked.

"Oh, a bit of all three I should expect," said Dad cheerfully. "Which reminds me, did Nathalia tell you about the time she thought the kettle was haunted?"

"Shuddup, Dad," hissed Nat.

Obviously he didn't shuddup, and Nat had to endure the story all over again.

"…Turns out it was just a faulty plug!" laughed Dad, finishing his tale. "But she still won't make a cup of tea after nine o'clock at night."

"Thought you didn't believe in ghosts?" said Darius. Nat looked for something heavy to brain Dad with.

The van groaned to a halt as they pulled up in front of Darius's little house. The garden, as usual, was full of rubbish.

"This garden looks like the inside of your head," Nat said to Dad.

Parked next to the house was a large black

van with pictures of corpses playing musical instruments all over it. In big bloody red letters someone had painted the words:

My Filthy Granny

"Has the circus come to your house?" asked Dad.

Darius was very quiet. He didn't seem to want to get out.

Dad thought for a minute and said: "You going to invite us in for a cup of tea then?"

Nat thought he'd gone mad. *What was Dad thinking?* No one went for a cup of tea at Oswald Bagley's house. An evening of mayhem and animal sacrifices, maybe, but not PG Tips. But Dad was already walking down the path, arm round Darius. Nat followed warily.

Inside the small, dark sitting room it looked like a meeting of the Zombie Council of Great Britain. Five scrawny young men, all dressed in black with white faces, blood-red lips and green-tinged eyes, lolled around drinking out of cans. Oswald grunted when he saw his younger brother and nodded at Dad and Nat. He didn't speak.

One of the creatures grabbed Darius playfully, though it was a bit rough for Nat's liking. "Here's our other little roadie. Where you been – *school*?" There was something sneery and unpleasant in his voice. Darius was smiling but Nat knew it wasn't a real smile.

Nat saw a poster lying on the floor. It read:

On tour – My Filthy Granny. Heavier than heavy metal, blacker than black metal, thrashier than thrash metal, speedier than speed metal, deader than death metal.

There were a bunch of dates in towns whose names Nat didn't recognise, but guessed were in Norway. So this is what Darius meant.

"A band, are you?" said Dad. The Grannies stopped throwing Darius about and turned bloodshot eyes towards him. "I used to play all the time..." Dad burbled on. "Course, I was a bit thinner in those days."

Nat began to get that familiar nasty creeping sensation down the back of her neck and in her stomach – the sign that her dad was about to be horribly embarrassing.

"I've got something in the van you'll like," he said, jumping up and running out the front door. The Grannies turned their pale faces to Nat. She tried to think of something to say that wouldn't get her eaten. She started with Darius. "You never said your brother was in a band."

"He's not," said the drummer, who used to be called Simon but apparently was now known as Dirty McNasty. "Oswald's our security." Oswald cracked his knuckles. Nat thought that he was probably there to stop the audience leaving.

"Oswald AND little Darius," said Mr McNasty. "You're coming wiv us too, ain't ya?" he said. "We all have a lot of – love – for little Darius." He cuffed Darius round the head lovingly enough to make his eyes wobble.

"Don't go asking for no autographs," said the singer, Derek Vomit, to Nat, unnecessarily. "You don't get no autographs, unless you get a tattoo of us. Shows you're a real fan. We're giving Darius one when we get to Oslo."

"Listen to this," said Dad, coming back in, holding a tiny, pink ukulele. It looked like a guitar that hadn't grown up yet. Nat felt sick. "I wrote this song ages ago. It was very popular down the student union bar. I was quite the rocker."

Nat wanted to hide under a cushion but it was unpleasant enough sitting ON a Bagley cushion; you would not want to be *under* one.

"Feel free to join in on the chorus, lads," said Dad, plunking tunelessly away. He LOVED meeting fellow musicians. "You'll probably want to use it at one of your gigs."

Nat knew there was only one thing worse than Dad playing the ukulele. It was Dad singing. Dad started singing.

"*I am a rocker*," he started, surprisingly loudly. And unsurprisingly flat. "*I am a shocker. You be the door and I'll be the knocker…*"

Oswald and the Filthy Grannies stared at the warbling idiot, grinning. Nat immediately saw they were nasty grins, but Dad took it for encouragement and sang louder.

"Let's have a go," said the guitarist, whose mum knew him as Jason but who was now called Stinky Gibbon. Dad handed him the uke. Stinky played a couple of notes and there was a crunching noise as he deliberately broke the neck off. "Oops, sorry!" he said, laughing. He handed Dad the smashed instrument back. "That's rock and roll for you."

Dad took the mashed instrument and thought for a moment.

"You're taking Darius with you this summer, are you?" he said to Oswald. There was a bit of steel in Dad's voice that Nat hardly recognised. Oswald nodded.

"Well, you're not," said Dad. "He's coming with us."

Nat couldn't be sure, but she thought that under his horrible black beard, Oswald Bagley smiled.

CHAPTER THREE

• • • •

IT WAS THE SATURDAY AFTER SCHOOL HAD FINISHED AND Nat and Dad were outside the house, packing the Atomic Dustbin. This first involved *un*-packing the Atomic Dustbin, as it was always full of junk. It was crammed with the stuff Dad liked that Mum wouldn't let in the house. So anyone walking past their drive that morning would have seen a rubbish van parked next to a rubbish *tip*. Nat had a baseball cap pulled down as far over her face as possible, in case anyone who knew her walked by.

Dad wasn't wearing a baseball cap; he thought baseball caps looked stupid. He was wearing an old T-shirt with 'Little Monkeys' written on it. Underneath was printed a photo of Nat, aged four, holding a monkey in a safari park. Nat was pulling a face because the chimp had just poked her in the eye. Dad thought the picture was cute, hence the T-shirt. Nat did not think it was cute, hence she'd thrown it in the bin fourteen times. But it still kept appearing. *Next time*, she thought darkly, *I'm setting fire to it. Even if Dad's wearing it.*

But even worse than the T-shirt were Dad's shorts. Dad wore shorts from June 1st to August 31st, because, he said, *that was summer*. He didn't wear them at any other time, no matter how hot, and he never wore anything else in the summer, no matter how cold or rainy. Dad was very proud of his shorts because he'd had them AT SCHOOL and he could still get into them. They were red and shiny and very *very* short. Way too short. From a distance it looked like he'd just forgotten to put his trousers on. Old ladies walked past the drive tutting and shielding their eyes.

Dad had extremely thin white hairy legs and in these shorts you could see ALL of those thin white hairy legs, from ankle to unmentionable. He bent over in the van and made it worse. Nat heard shrieks from the other side of the street and had to hide behind the Dog.

To top it all, Dad had the radio on. Fighting over the radio was becoming what writers of modern classics would call: AN ISSUE. In the old days, Nat didn't care what awful music Dad listened to, because she was still finding out what music she liked. But now she was older and had found out what she liked and it was the music they played on RADIO ZINGG!!! It was happy bouncy music you could dance to. Dad liked RADIO DAD. The songs on RADIO DAD went on for hours and if you tried to dance to them you'd break your legs. They were boring and miserable and now it was playing at full blast and all the neighbours would think that *she* liked Dave Spong and his Incredible Flaming Earwigs, or whoever it was.

Because of all this, Nat was very keen to get the van cleared and packed so they could get out of there. But the more Dad chucked out on to the drive, the more there was still inside. It was like some evil van curse.

Normal families fly abroad on holiday, thought Nat sourly, dragging more cases to the van. But Dad kept telling them it would be 'more fun' (in other words, *cheaper*) to drive there instead.

"We'll need a car when we get there *anyway*," he had argued to Mum. "And this saves us the expense of hiring one. Plus, we'll make a holiday of the journey. We can sleep in the van. Or there's a big old tent in the back. You like camping!"

This was not true. Mum hated camping. Mum liked hotels and hot water and fluffy towels and chocolates on the pillow and room service. She did not like:

Tents, campsites, bugs, sleeping bags, burnt

sausages, shared showers, smelly loos, rain, fetching water from a pipe in a field, cows, hippies, wet socks, and any of the four great smells of camping – plastic, burnt wood, damp dirt and wee.

This wasn't the reason she gave though. Mum would have to miss the whole camping bit because *obviously*, she said, she couldn't get a month off work. "Unlike your father, who rarely gets a month ON work."

Mum usually got upset when she missed out on family time, but Nat was pretty sure Mum was relieved to be missing out on the camping part of the trip.

Instead, the plan was that Dad, Nat and Darius would take the van over to France, and when Mum could get away she would fly out to join them, probably towards the end, and once Dad had found her a nice hotel nearby.

"But you can just stay in the house! I'll have it done up by the time you arrive," Dad had argued.

"Now, I don't mean to be critical, love," Mum had pointed out, "but you're not a builder. You write jokes for Christmas crackers. I have no idea why you've agreed to do all this work. The last time you tried to put up a bookshelf you nailed your head to a copy of *Great Expectations*."

Dad had mumbled something about it being a bit quiet on the Christmas cracker-joke-writing job front at the moment and that it might be good for him to develop another skill or two. Mum had just smiled and kissed him and reminded him to take out extra health insurance and a first-aid kit.

"Do you think we'll need this?" Dad asked Nat, emerging backwards from the depths of the van, waving an electric pencil sharpener.

"No idea, Dad, I've got my eyes closed," shouted Nat, burying her face in the Dog's warm fur. "Please change your shorts."

Whatever Dad said next was drowned out by the roar of a huge motorcycle engine. Oswald had arrived with Darius sitting on the back of the bike. The Dog bounded up, sure of a treat. Darius hopped off and picked some flies out of his teeth. He was carrying a small tatty rucksack. It didn't look big enough to hold a decent packed lunch, let alone anything else.

"Is that all you're bringing?" asked Nat.

"It's all I've got," Darius replied lightly, before getting bundled over by the excited Dog. The two of them rolled around in the front garden. Oswald nodded to Dad, revved his motorbike and sped off without saying goodbye to his little brother. Dad watched him go for a moment, then turned to Darius. "Best say goodbye to the mutt," he said, "we're taking him to the kennels later."

Nat was shocked. "Dad—" she began.

"I know what you're going to say," he said, cutting her off, "but he'll hate that long drive and he won't like strange places and Mum's too busy to look after him. He'll be better off in a kennel, trust me. I've picked a nice one."

Nat wasn't one to take no for an answer. "Mum…" she shouted, running indoors.

Mum was on her mobile and doing emails at the same time. Nat wanted to tell her why she HAD to have the Dog with her and that Mum HAD to make Dad understand but didn't want to interrupt so, after hovering nearby for a few minutes, she went upstairs and threw herself on the bed in misery.

Which is where she was when Bad News Nan came looking for her.

"Your fasher said you washn't feeling very well," she said, showering Nat with biscuit crumbs. Her voice was muffled due to the addition of digestives and the lack of teeth. Bad News Nan often kept her false teeth in her pocket so as not to wear them out by over-use. Many an evening at home had been livened up by the sudden discovery of Nan's gnashers under a cushion.

Or in the dishwasher.

Or in the biscuit tin.

Or in the butter dish.

"It's just Dad," grumbled Nat, "and this stupid holiday. It's going to be a typical Dad disaster, I know it. And if I haven't got the Dog, there'll be no one to have a sensible conversation with."

Bad News Nan had stopped listening after the word 'disaster'. She liked nothing better than a good disaster. "Well, if you think *your* life's bad…" she began, and proceeded to tell Nat about:

Edna Pudding – lost two fingers in the bacon slicer at Morrison's.

Deidre Scratchnsniff – put winning lottery ticket through a hot wash.

Frank Mealtime – took a pedalo out too far at Camber Sands and was captured by Somali pirates. His niece had to put all her bone china figurines on eBay to pay the ransom.

Nat wasn't too sure how true any of these were (especially the Edna story, because the last time she'd seen Mrs Pudding she was working on the checkouts, not the deli counter), but funnily enough, they did make her feel a bit better.

"I've told your father this whole expedition is stupid," she droned on. "I said little Nat should just come and stay with me this summer. Would you like that?"

Nat hesitated. On the one hand, Bad News Nan was completely mad and never stopped talking or eating unless she was asleep, and even then kept going sometimes. Nat knew she would be forced to listen to all the hard-luck stories that Nan collected the way Mum collected parking tickets. On the other hand, having no Dad to show her up sounded pretty amazing, and she could hang out with Penny Posnitch who lived round the corner from Nan. She could make a few new friends and maybe move up the popularity ladder at least TWO RUNGS.

And besides that, there would be NOTHING TO DO at Nan's except do what Nan did – get up at lunchtime, watch endless episodes of *Judge Judy*, and never eat a vegetable again. On balance – it sounded brilliant.

Only one problem.

"How about Darius and the Dog?" Nat asked.

"I'm not looking after them," said Nan firmly. "They'd both have to go in kennels."

Nat sighed and reluctantly pushed herself off the bed. France it was. But she was NOT putting the Dog in kennels. She just needed a plan.

CHAPTER FOUR

• • • •

AT LAST THE VAN WAS CLEARED OF ALL ITS RUBBISH and repacked with slightly more useful rubbish, and it was time for everyone to say their goodbyes. Mum gave Nat an extra squeezy hug.

"Can I stay here and get a job in your office instead?" whispered Nat, only half joking.

Mum grinned. "Yes, I wish we could swap places. But look, you're going to a foreign country with your idiot father and demon child Darius Bagley in a horrible van to rebuild a haunted house. Think how lucky you are!"

Sometimes, thought Nat, *Mum's sense of humour is as bad as Dad's.*

"Right, let's go. Where's the Dog?" said Dad, looking sweaty and harassed.

Somewhere in the Dog's tiny doggie brain he must have sensed something was up, because they found him trembling under a pile of dirty washing. Dad had to carry him out to the van, still tangled up in the sheets and looking utterly pathetic. He turned his sad brown dog eyes to Mum as he was carried to the van, as if to say, "Are you doing this to me too?"

"In, in, let's go," said Dad to Nat and Darius as he slammed the door and started the engine. Or rather, *tried* to start the engine. It coughed and banged and wheezed and went silent.

Mum waved her arms, exasperated. "You said you'd get this horrible old thing ready for the road!" she said. "How do you expect it to carry you across half of France if you can't get it off the drive?"

"We can't go! We have to stay here, what a

shame, never mind," shouted Nat as she scrambled out of the van, her heart leaping with joy.

"Nothing I can't fix," said Dad, hopping out. He lifted the bonnet and leaned right over to get at the engine. There was a scream from Mrs Possett opposite at number 26 who wished she hadn't chosen that moment to stand at the window and take her net curtains down.

"You could stop Dad going," Nat said urgently to Mum, out of earshot, "he does what you tell him."

"No, he doesn't," said Mum, pleased at the thought all the same, "but anyway, it'll be good for him to fix this silly house and prove to everyone round here he's not *totally* daft and useless."

But he is, thought Nat.

There was muffled clanging and swearing from under the bonnet for about five minutes, until Darius jumped out of the van, holding some kind of multitool he'd taken from his rucksack. "Let's have a look," he said to Dad. "I've fixed Oswald's bike loads of times."

Dad slapped him on the back and walked over to Mum. "See," he said, "no problem. Darius is going to mend it."

"He's just a little boy, you moron!" yelled Mum. "You ARE daft and useless."

Told you, thought Nat.

By now there was quite a crowd gathering on the pavement to watch what was going on. The neighbours knew there was always something fun to watch at Nat's house. A lot of them preferred it to the telly. Nat and the Dog got back in the van and hid.

"But he's brilliant with his hands," said Dad cheerfully. "Who do you think fixed our washing machine last month?"

In the van, Nat cringed. Even she knew Dad had just made a massive mistake. Mum grabbed the nearest object from the pile of junk that had been chucked out of the van. It happened to be a rude garden gnome that Dad once thought was funny. Now he just thought it looked heavy and sharp. She advanced on Dad dangerously. He smartly backed off, towards the small crowd, who were really getting their money's worth today.

"You said you got an engineer out," she said quietly. Nat got worried. Most people get louder as they get angrier, but not Mum. She started off loud, then got quieter. She was deadly quiet now.

"Be fair, love, he did a great job, and he was much cheaper than a real engineer. You can pay him in Mars bars and Pringles."

Dad had also discovered that if you gave Darius enough fizzy orange pop he worked twice as quickly, but interestingly, Mum got even madder when he told her that.

Nat watched through her fingers as the rude gnome went whistling past Dad's left ear and took out Mister Sponge who was peeping over the privet. He went down like a sack of bricks, but whatever he shouted was lost as the van roared to life, sounding louder and healthier than ever. Darius, face covered in oil, gave them a thumbs up and a huge smile from the driver's seat.

"Darius, right, get out of that seat, shut the

bonnet, get in the back, quick," shouted Dad, slamming the door. "Bye, love, sorry, have to dash, love you, gotta catch the ferry, bye!" And they were off, scattering the neighbours as they went.

By the time they got to the kennels, the Dog had licked all the oil off Darius and Dad noticed he had a lot of texts from Mum on his mobile. He wouldn't let Nat see them, but she did manage to glimpse a few of the words. One or two were completely new to her. She made a mental note to ask Darius about them when Dad wasn't listening.

They were now in the leafy bit of town where the kennels were. It was the bit of town that pretended to be countryside, even though there was now a massive busy road going right through it, and a kebab shop and off-licence on almost every corner.

Soon they turned down a driveway with a big sign saying 'Pawlty Towers'. Mournful howling resounded from behind large dark hedges. The woman who came to meet them at the front gate was middle-aged and built like a huge Saint Bernard dog. Nat sniggered when she said her name was Bernadette. The lady shot her a stern glance.

Bernadette wore a quilted green jacket and horse-riding trousers, even though Nat couldn't see a horse anywhere. She took one look at Nat's miserable dog – who was being carried out of the van, bundled up in the bed sheets like a pile of wet washing – and turned up her nose.

"Well, we usually only take pedigrees," she said. "On the phone you said he was a pedigree." Nat looked at Dad. *Here we go again*, she thought. Dad would say anything to try and get his own way.

"Did I?" he remarked innocently. "I think I said there was some pedigree IN him. Would you not call him a pedigree then?"

"No, this is what we in the dog business call a *mutt*," said Bernadette. She was going to say a lot more but just then Dad hoisted the Dog higher and she suddenly got an eyeful of the shorts. "Oh my goodness," she muttered. "Oh dear me." She went red and quickly turned round. "Yes, well, there is one space. I'll lead the way. DO NOT walk in front of me."

As they trudged up the gravel path, past the cages full of dogs, all now barking like mad, Nat whispered to Darius: "Right, remember what we planned." Darius looked blank. "The plan," said Nat. "*My plan* to rescue the Dog. The plan I planned. It's all planned. I told you the—"

"Nah, I've got a better plan, Buttface," interrupted Darius, hopping over cracks in the pavement.

Nat fumed. "You have NOT got a plan!" she hissed. "You never have a plan. You just do the first thing that comes into your head. That's why you get on with Dad. He's the same. A big chimp, like you."

She did an impression of Dad crossed with a monkey: "Oh look, a banana, think I'll eat it. Oh no, now here's a coconut, yum yum, ooh and now there's a tyre, I'll swing on that. Now, what was

I doing with that banana? No idea, because I'm a chimp, ooh ooh."

"Is that girl all right in the head?" said Bernadette. "Can you get her to stop making animal noises? She's upsetting the dogs."

"Just do the plan, chimpy," said Nat. "MY plan."

Nat's plan was really complicated. She'd not had a lot of time to think about it. If she'd have had MORE time maybe she'd have made it simpler, but either way, this was Nat's plan:

They get to the kennel door.

Darius pretends to have a terrible sudden illness, involving general agonised thrashing about and foaming at the mouth (Darius liked this bit).

While everyone's looking after Darius, Nat steals the keys to the kennels.

Nat finds a dog that looks just like her dog, and frees it.

Nat gives Darius a secret signal to stop thrashing/foaming.

They give the lookalike dog to the kennel lady,

who locks it up.

They hide Nat's dog under the blanket and escape with him back to the car.

But when they got to the cage, Darius refused to pretend to be ill, no matter how hard Nat pinched him. The kennel lady unlocked the door. The Dog whimpered and jumped into Darius's arms. Still Darius just stood there. Finally, in desperation, Nat threw herself on the ground and began shouting:

"Oh the pain, the pain. It's at the very least rabies. Help."

To her fury, everyone ignored her. Dad was filling out a form and Bernadette had already decided Nat was a silly little thing and best ignored. It was hopeless. Nat really DID feel like thrashing about, but in frustration. *This is all Bagley's fault*, she thought. *He's ruined my perfect plan.*

Then Darius did something strange. He threw the keys to the Atomic Dustbin on the path just behind Dad. "You've dropped the keys," he said.

"Thanks," said Dad, bending right over to

pick them up. Bernadette made a strangled sort of being-sick noise and turned her back to them, sharpish.

At that moment, Darius shoved the Dog's empty bed sheets into the cage and thrust the actual Dog at Nat, whispering: "Hide him."

Inside the cage all you could see was the bundle of washing. As far as anyone could tell, the Dog could still have been wrapped up in it. He wasn't, of course; because by now Nat was stuffing him under the table in the van and giving him one of Dad's socks to chew quietly.

By the time Dad had straightened up again and Bernadette had opened her eyes, she had had quite enough of this weird family and quickly finished off the paperwork, locking the cage door without really looking and shooing them all off her property.

Nat was in the back of the van when Dad and Darius returned. "Sorry, love," said Dad. "It's for the best."

Nat nodded. Under the table, covered in tea

towels, was the Dog. He probably nodded too.

Nat didn't speak to Darius again until it was dark and they were nearly at the ferry terminal. "Anyway, well done. My plan was better, though..." she finally muttered.

Darius didn't say anything because he was trying to stretch a bogey longer than anyone had ever stretched a bogey before. The Dog didn't say anything because he was rather hoping to eat the bogey.

"You just got lucky," Nat went on. "Even my dad's plans are better than yours and he's a moron."

At that moment Dad slammed on the handbrake. He turned round. "Probably should have thought of this before," he said, with a sort of laugh, "but, um, you HAVE got your passport with you, haven't you, Darius?"

Darius's face was blank. His bogey snapped and slapped on the table.

"Told you so," said Nat.

CHAPTER FIVE

• • • •

THEY WERE SITTING IN THE QUEUE OF CARS AND vans and lorries to get on the next ferry. It was now properly dark and the ferry terminal, lit by huge white lamps, looked misty and spooky. Men and women in high-visibility jackets walked around on the concrete, acting fierce. Dad had just borrowed Nat's phone to call Darius's brother, Oswald, as his didn't seem to be working. Nat thought Dad should be in a massive panic but he just looked mildly confused. Like he always did.

"So, according to Oswald," Dad said, "you've

never even HAD a passport. Oswald said something about not believing in them. He thinks people should be able to go where and do whatever they want and everyone else can go and get, er –" Dad paused – "get lost, was the general idea. At least I *think* that's what he said, because there was some kind of explosion taking place nearby."

"That'll be the Grannies," said Darius.

"Why, do their songs sound like explosions?" asked Nat.

"No," said Darius, "they just like blowing things up."

"Right," said Dad. "Anyway, I asked how you'd have got into Norway with them without a passport. He said you just fitted nicely inside a big amplifier."

"Yeah, I do," said Darius.

"Interesting." Dad paused for a few seconds, sucking on a mint. "So I suppose you could fit inside a…" Dad looked around for something to hide Darius in.

"Dad, you can't!" shouted Nat, realising with

horror what Dad was thinking of doing. "We have to go back NOW. Smuggling a dog is one thing, but smuggling people is really bad. I saw a documentary on it. On Blue Peter."

"Smuggling a dog?" said Dad. "What dog?"

Nat put her hand over her mouth, but it was too late. Then the Dog, who'd been quiet long enough, gave a short bark as if to say, "THIS dog, stupid."

"Blooming heck, love, you'll get us shot," said Dad mildly. "There's all sorts of laws about taking dogs out of the country."

"Dogs AND PEOPLE!" shouted Nat, attracting the attention of one of the men in the yellow jackets, who glanced over at the van. She lowered her voice. "We'll all go to prison and I don't care what Nan says, I don't think prisons are very nice."

Bad News Nan always said that when she got REALLY old, instead of going into a cheapo old people's home, she was going to rob a post office and with a bit of luck she'd get sent to prison.

She said the food was better in the nick, there were bigger TVs and the people inside were more interesting. She also said she couldn't lose because if she got away with the post office hold-up then she'd be rich enough to afford a nice old people's home with huge TVs and endless Hobnobs.

This made Nat very nervous every time she went to the post office with her. She'd always try and sneak a look inside Nan's handbag just in case she was hiding a black balaclava and some kind of offensive weapon. Luckily, up till now, the only offensive thing Nat had found in Nan's handbag were her teeth.

"Well, let's be sensible," said Dad. These words always terrified Nat. Dad's version of sensible was NOT anyone else's. "It takes weeks to get a passport, and it would involve loads of important paperwork that we'd need to find at Darius's house, and I don't think Oswald is a paperwork kind of person."

"That's true," said Darius. "He's more of a setting-fire-to-paperwork kind of person."

Nat knew this to be true. Oswald liked setting fire to Darius's school books, for instance.

"So," said Dad, "given I've paid for these ferry tickets now, the sensible thing to do is carry on."

"That's not *sensible*, Dad," she yelled, "that's ILLEGAL AND WRONG!"

But Dad had already disappeared into the back of the van and was rummaging through the junk. He eventually reappeared with a great big picnic basket.

"Oh right," said Nat, "let's all have a ham sandwich and a pork pie. That'll make it better." Dad ignored her and started chucking out all the crockery. When it was empty, he eyed up Darius. "In you get, lad," he said. "It's literally the only option."

"It literally is *not* the only option, Dad," argued Nat, as Darius clambered in. "It's literally the most terrible of all the options you could choose."

"Except swimming across the channel," said Darius from inside the hamper. "That's a more terrible option."

"Don't give him ideas," said Nat, watching Dad's face as he thought about it.

"Can you squeeze the Dog in with you?" asked Dad, chucking it at Darius regardless.

"Just about," said Darius.

And with that, Dad got back in the driver's seat. The ferry had begun to load and cars were moving. "Just don't make a noise," Dad shouted over the noise of the engine.

"OK, but the Dog's breath really smells," said Darius.

Nat broke into a proper cold sweat when they drove up to the customs window and Dad handed over their two passports. *You've really done it this time, Dad*, she thought. Visiting your dad in prison was embarrassing, but being in prison WITH him was something else.

It seemed to take forever for the bored border guard to flick through the passports.

"Bum hole?" he said eventually, with the first smile he'd cracked all year. "Is this a wind-up?"

Nat went red. It didn't matter how many times she heard it…

"It's pronounced *bew-mow-lay*, actually," said Dad. "It's old and French. There are the Paris Bumolés, the Lille Bumolés, and I think there are some Nice Bumolés down south."

"France is full of Bumolés, is it?" sniggered the border guard. "I thought so."

Finally, after he'd finished laughing, their van was waved on to the ferry.

"That's another big fat stress wrinkle in my forehead you've given me, Dad," complained Nat when they were safely parked inside the hold of the massive ship. "By the time I'm eighteen I'll look like a bulldog chewing a hot chip."

There was a snort of laughter from the picnic basket and Nat nearly had a heart attack. "SHUT UP, DARIUS!" she shouted. Really really loudly.

"Shush!" said Dad.

There was a gargling, choking sound from the basket. "Stop messing," said Nat, who was getting more and more nervous.

"I can't help it, the Dog's dropped one," said Darius in a voice that sounded like he was being strangled by a sweaty sock. This was terrible news. The Dog's guffs were legendary. He could clear a large room in seconds. Nat could only imagine what it must have been like in a tiny space. She started to giggle.

"Well, don't let it out," she said. "It's bound to smell horrible."

"It does!" said Darius, gasping for breath. "It's doing something weird to me. I'm starting to see things. Lemme out the basket."

"Soon," said Dad, watching all the passengers getting out of their cars. "We have to wait until the coast is clear." He sniffed. "Oh no, that is bad," he added. "We're even getting it out here."

"I'm going to be sick!" said Darius.

"Put your head between your knees," spluttered Nat, who couldn't stop giggling.

"It IS between my knees; how do you think I fit in the picnic basket?"

"Is everything all right?" said a voice suddenly. It was a member of the ship's crew, poking his nose in at the van window. "Everyone else has gone upstairs. You'll have missed the fish and chips at the cafeteria by now. Very popular is the fish and chips. Everything else is French muck."

The man peered into the van. He sniffed the air. "I dunno what's on your picnic menu tonight," he said, pulling a face, "but if I were you, I'd stick to crisps."

Dad laughed a pretend laugh. Even Nat could tell it was the kind of laugh that massively guilty people do when they're hiding something.

The man looked at them both.

"You have to get out, we're locking this cargo dock in five minutes."

"No problem," said Dad, not moving. "Bye."

But the man wasn't going anywhere. "And why do you keep shouting about a picnic basket?"

"Er – because we're very proud of it," said Dad. "We got it at a pound shop."

"How much was it?" said the crafty man, who was called Mick and had been trained to be suspicious. It had earned him his nickname.

"A tenner," said Dad without thinking, falling into the trap.

Nat put her head in her hands. *A tenner?* she thought. *From a POUND SHOP? Oh, Dad, we're doomed...*

"Ha! Oh really?" said Suspicious Mick happily. "I'm not sure about that. Not sure one little bit. Something's not right about this story. I think I want a look at this famous picnic basket."

There was nothing they could do. Their epic journey was over before it had even begun. Dad opened the slidy van door and Suspicious Mick took hold of the basket lid. He wafted the air, which was still smelling grim. "If you've got egg sandwiches in there, they're off," he said.

This is it, thought Nat. *I wonder if they have a prison cell on the ship or if they still make you walk the plank. Oh well, as long as I get to see Dad go overboard first. Hope there're sharks...*

Suspicious Mick lifted the lid.

"I can explain…" began Dad.

The basket was empty.

"Oh. No, I can't," said Dad.

CHAPTER SIX

• • • •

"LOOKING ON THE BRIGHT SIDE..." SAID DAD, AS he and Nat ran around the deck of the crowded ship looking for the missing Darius and the Dog, "he could always get a job in a circus. You know, escaping from things. You can get on telly doing that."

"There's no bright side if he's escaped right off this ferry and we never see him again," said Nat angrily, peeking under a lifeboat cover. "And that's not really a proper job anyway. You told me that joining a circus is NOT a proper job."

Dad thought for a moment. Nat watched as the bright lights on the deck showed up all the wrinkles in his forehead. "I remember that conversation," he said. "You said you wanted to be a lion tamer." A few passengers who had come outside to look at the sea began listening to their conversation.

Dad carried on. "You practised lion taming on next door's guinea pigs." An elderly couple in matching pink and blue anoraks looked at Nat and went "Aaaah" in that way old people in anoraks do.

"That's so sweet, isn't it, Ernie?" shouted the old lady to her husband, who was a bit deaf. "She started on guinea pigs." Dad turned to the couple, glad of a chance to talk about his wonderful little girl.

"Oh, but you don't know the best bit," Dad smiled.

"He said *you don't know the best bit*," shouted the old lady to her husband, loudly enough for him to hear, which meant loudly enough for everyone within fifty metres to hear as well.

Nat looked quickly around for somewhere to hide and made a note in her head to get Darius to teach HER how to disappear.

"She tried to lion-tame some cows in a field when we were having a picnic," Dad went on. "She spent an hour trying to get them to jump through a hula hoop."

Nat saw a little metal door with a sign on which read KEEP OUT – CREW ONLY. She tried the handle and found it wasn't locked. Nat hated breaking rules, but it was this or suffer yet another one of Dad's embarrassing tales about her, so... she opened the door and slipped quietly inside.

Out on deck, Dad was just getting to the best bit:

"Then the farmer came and shouted at her to stop bothering his cows as it would put them off milking. But when the cows saw him they thought it was time to get milked, so they started running towards him.

"Problem was, Nathalia was right in their

way. She realised they weren't going to stop. The farmer was shouting, she was screaming and running as fast as her tiny little skinny legs would carry her.

"Which wasn't that fast because she slipped in one cow pat and went face-first in another. It was soooooo funny!"

"He said *then the little girl went face-first in cow poo!*" shouted the old lady.

"Oh that IS funny, he's quite right," said the old man. "Is he part of the entertainment? Should we give him a tip?"

"It put her off lion-taming for life," said Dad, chuckling. He looked around for the star of his story. "Hmmm," he said. "Where's she gone?"

The room Nat was hiding in was small and dark. It was a kind of store room, full of stuff some people tell other people will be useful one day. Nat hadn't put the light on but she felt safe in the gloom – right until the moment someone tapped her on the shoulder and said:

"Boo."

She gave a shriek of fright and jumped about two feet in the air, landing with a crash on some boxes of Styrofoam cups. The box burst and the squeaky cups scattered on to the floor.

"Shush," said Darius, coming out of his hiding place, "you'll attract attention. If we were escaping from a prisoner of war camp, you'd have been shot by now."

Nat grabbed him by the hair. "It's not a machine-gun tower you need to worry about," she said. "It's being strangled by me."

They rolled around on the squeaky cups for a while, Nat getting in some good pinches and a fair amount of strangling, until the Dog jumped between them, licking them both into submission. Finally Nat let go and sat there, panting. "Do not creep up on me again," she said, chucking a pack of dishcloths at his head. "Anyway, how did you escape without being seen?"

"It was easy," he replied, rubbing his bruises. "I'm pretty good at getting out of small dark places. I've had tons of practice." Not for the first time, Nat suddenly felt sorry for her friend, and went from wanting to murder him to wanting to hug him. She HATED the way he did that to her, so she bashed him with a mop.

Before she could say anything more, Dad popped his head round the door. "You in here, love?" he said. "There are loads of people outside who want to meet the famous cow-tamer."

The Dog bounded out to him, and then Dad noticed Darius. "Oh, we wondered where you'd got to," he said cheerfully. "Come on, the canteen's open. Last chance for pork pies and pickled eggs before Paris." He looked the boy up and down briefly, making sure he was in one piece, then they all trundled off for something to eat and that was that.

One of the few things Nat ever admitted she liked about her idiot dad was that he wasn't one of those 'asking-loads-of-difficult-questions' dads. He just got on with it. And went to buy a pork pie and a pickled egg.

"They don't sell these in Europe!" said Dad

defensively, as Nat told him off for coming back with his THIRD pork pie slice from the ferry canteen. The Dog was now safely hidden in their van, giving them all a chance to relax and enjoy the 'delicious and delightful' canteen food.

There is a rule everyone should know which says that the **nicer** the words in a menu are, the more **horrid** the food will be. For example, if you read something which says:

'Delicious tender fish gently coaxed from the sea and enrobed in mouth-tingling crispy crumb batter, served sizzling on an enticing bed of fluffy *petits pois*, encircled by gorgeously ruffled hand-carved wedges of majestic potato...'

...it'll be rank.

"These fish and chips are rank, Dad," moaned Nat, "and it said on the menu they would be delicious." There was a huge burp. "Oh, I see you've finished," she said to Darius primly.

"Don't you want the rest of yours?" said Darius, wiping tomato ketchup from his chin with his sleeve. Nat pushed her plate over to him.

"OK, so here's the plan," said Dad. Nat looked at him, puzzled. Dad never planned anything. But now he unfolded a huge map across the table, along with lots of bits of paper. And pens. And bits of string, receipts, bus tickets, packets of sugar, some lego bricks, pocket fluff and paper clips.

Some French kids on the next table started pointing. Nat tried to ignore them.

"We should get back to our cabin and get some sleep now," said Dad, as Darius scraped tomato sauce off the map with a knife and sucked it clean. "Tomorrow we get into France…"

"Unless we get caught smuggli— ah ha hoo ha nothing," burbled Nat, who out of the corner of her eye had spotted Suspicious Mick, walking past with a tray of rank fish and chips. Nat grabbed the map and held it over her face.

"I've worked out a route to the farmhouse," Dad continued, putting the map down on to the table and into a splodge of tomato ketchup. Nat looked at the map and saw that he had just taken a red felt tip and drawn a straight line from the ferry terminal all the way to where Posh Barry's rubbish damp haunted house was.

"The quickest distance between two points is a straight line," Dad explained. "So we'll just go on the roads that are *nearest* the line. It'll save time."

"Stupid idea," said a voice over his shoulder. Nat froze.

It was Suspicious Mick. "Why's that then?" asked Dad. Mick pulled up a chair and sat down without being asked. Darius slid under the table. Nat watched as a grubby hand came up, grabbed the rest of her freshly battered fish and disappeared under the table again.

Dad did not like people in uniform. He often told Nat that they made him feel like he had something to hide, even when he didn't. Obviously this time he DID have something to hide. But did that mean that Dad would keep a low profile? Oh no, nothing that sensible. Nat guessed what was coming: an argument. She was right.

"It's not ridiculous, it's genius," argued Dad.

Suspicious Mick snorted. "I can tell you're not a REAL driver. A REAL driver would take the road from…"

Nat listened to the man drone on endlessly about roads and roundabouts and routes and, not for the first time, wished she could press a 'fast-forward' button on bits of her life.

Dad obviously felt the same. He had a very short attention span at the best of times. Finally he'd had enough. He stood up. "Right," said Dad. "I'll show you who's the better driver. Come to the video arcade. If you're not too scared." Nat put her head on the table and tried not to cry.

Suspicious Mick realised he was being watched by a bunch of bored French kids so now he could not back down.

When they reached the arcade, trailed by the now not-bored French kids (and with Darius following at a safe distance), they found two big racing car machines, side by side.

"This won't prove anything," said Suspicious Mick. "It's childish."

That's my Dad! thought Nat. *Took you long enough.*

"Bwark bwark bwark," said Dad, making chicken noises, and doing that thing with his head and elbows. The French kids laughed.

Nat tugged at Dad's sleeve. "Don't upset him," she whispered. "He might get us into trouble."

But Dad was enjoying himself now. "Come on, Mick, get in," he said. "Or should I call you MICK NUGGET?"

"McNUGGET!" laughed the French kids. One nudged Nat. "Eet's funny becawse 'is name is Mick and 'e's ze chicken," he explained.

"Yes, I know," she said crossly. "I get *le joke*. It's just a bad one. Like all Dad's jokes. Stop encouraging him."

Now the two men were in their cars. They put their money in and the race clock counted down. FIVE... FOUR...

"Last one to finish has to run through the ship with their pants on their head!" shouted Dad.

Nat froze. Dad was a REALLY SLOW driver.

And he always got lost. He was bound to lose.

THREE…

Worse, he was wearing his 'Little Monkeys' T-shirt again. So the whole boat would know the pants-head man was her dad.

TWO…

"You're on!" shouted Suspicious Mick over the noise of the electronic engines and the chanting children.

"Pants pants pants!" they shouted. "Head head head!"

Nat noticed that Darius was leading the chanting.

ONE.

And they were off.

CHAPTER SEVEN

• • • •

BY THE END OF LAP ONE DAD WAS ALREADY LOSING.

"Put your foot down, Dad!" yelled Nat. "You're going to be Pants Head if you don't catch him soon."

Suspicious Mick was concentrating hard. He had EVERYTHING clenched: teeth, fingers, buttocks. Truth is, he was a clenched kind of person to begin with. He had played this game loads over the years. He often chucked children off the machine to get a free go.

He knew all the bits to speed on and where

to brake. He even knew the cheaty short cuts. Nat watched in despair as Suspicious Mick slid sideways round a nasty bend and went through a wall of tyres on to another bit of track, saving a good ten seconds. Meanwhile, Dad carefully changed down into second gear to avoid running into a pigeon. He was DOOMED.

Suspicious Mick hit the throttle on a long straight. The car roared and surged forward. The stupid animated fans on the machine cheered as the real audience booed. But wait... Something weird was happening. Mick was heading for a hairpin bend at a ridiculous speed. He was going TOO FAST. Surely he couldn't take that bend this fast, thought Nat.

No, he couldn't. He was jabbing his foot on the brake pedal but nothing was happening. With a yell he tried to turn the wheel, but it was too late. His car ploughed into a bank of spectators in the biggest crash anyone had ever seen. The screen erupted in cartoon flame.

The French kids cheered. Mick frantically

reversed. Dad was starting to gain on him. Mick roared off, Dad now only two cars behind. The same crazy thing happened again; Mick got faster and faster, crashing into barrier after barrier, metal shrieking and sparks flying.

But he was still just in front as the finish line came in sight. But it was close – Dad was right behind him. "Come on, Dad," shouted Nat, "put your blinking foot down!"

The chequered flag went up, signalling the end of the race was nigh. It went down on…

Mick's car! He had won.

Mick jumped up. "Beat you, beat you, ha ha ha," he shouted nastily. The kids booed like he was a panto villain. "Pants on your head, get them on!" crowed Mick heartlessly.

Nat felt sick. Dad was going to break all previous embarrassment records. But no. What was this? A computerised referee appeared on the screen, wagging a finger at Mick's car.

Stern text appeared.

"Due to dangerous driving, this car has been

given a ten-second time penalty. The winner of the race is now – car number two."

Dad had won!

The French kids went *wild*. Dad did a victory lap of the arcade as Nat cringed and Mick slunk off saying he had to get back to work and the machine was broken and it wasn't fair and he never wanted to see any of them ever again and no he WASN'T going to wear his pants on his head for anyone, thank you, so there.

"Bad loser, bad loser," sang the chorus of kids behind him. He shook his fist at them and went off to shout at the smallest people he could find.

Nat breathed a sigh of relief. She knew Dad would DEFINITELY have worn his pants on his head if *he'd* lost. *He might just do it anyway*, she thought glumly, *just cos he'll think it's funny*.

"Let's go to our cabin and go to bed," said Dad, after he'd stopped offering to sign autographs. "Then when we wake up we'll be in another country. That's exciting."

Darius trotted off behind him and Nat was

just about to follow when she noticed something colourful by the machine that Suspicious Mick had been driving. When she looked closer, she noticed that something was stuck under the brake pedal.

It was a dog's thick rubber chew toy.

It was *her* dog's thick rubber chew toy.

She caught up with Darius just as he was about to go into the cabin. She gave him the toy. He looked at it, expressionless.

"Any idea how this got under the brake pedal?" she asked.

Darius just shrugged.

The cabin was tiny and hot, with a small porthole looking out over the dark water. They were near the ferry's huge engines, which hummed and made the room vibrate. Nat found it hard to sleep, worrying about the two passport-less creatures opposite. What if they were caught and thrown in a French jail? And even if they didn't get caught, then there was a whole mad journey ahead, with only a rotten, falling-down, haunted house at the end of it.

In the middle of the night, listening to the engines, Dad's snoring, the Dog's dreamy whimpers and Darius's mutterings, Nat decided she had to do SOMETHING useful. So she threw Dad's red shorts out of the porthole. She slept a lot better after that.

They woke about an hour before the ferry got into port. "I suppose we'll need some sort of plan," said Dad, looking at Darius and the Dog.

Darius shrugged. "Nah," he said, "something'll turn up."

Dad brightened. "Yeah, I'm sure you're right," he agreed. "Now, who wants breakfast?"

Nathalia couldn't believe it. *Surely, if ever there was need for a plan, then trying to smuggle a boy and a dog into a foreign country where there are proper big laws against that sort of thing was THE TIME FOR A FLIPPING PLAN*, she thought.

Down in the canteen, plan-less Nat watched helplessly through the window as the ferry terminal slid into view.

"*Could all car passengers please make their way to the car deck as we are about to arrive. Have a good holiday,*" said the voice over the Tannoy.

A good holiday sounds amazing, thought Nat. *This isn't one though.* She grabbed Dad as they made their way to the van. "It's not too late. Let's turn ourselves in and throw ourselves on the mercy of the— ah hoo ha hoo ha nothing."

Suspicious Mick, back in his high visibility jacket, was striding towards them. Dad was carrying what looked like the biggest bag of booze in the world. In fact it was the Dog, wrapped up and hidden in a Duty Free bag.

Suspicious Mick looked at the parcel. "Like a drink, do we?" he said.

"Presents," said Dad. "I thought I'd get them here. They don't sell wine where we're going."

"France?" said Mick. "They do. They do sell wine in France."

"I've been misinformed then," said Dad.

"There's something not quite right about you,"

said Mick. "I just can't put my finger on it." He jabbed his finger at the parcel Dad was carrying. The Dog yelped.

"Shush, Nat," said Dad hastily. "She has this problem. It makes her yelp. We don't like to talk about it." Mick looked at Nat.

Nat yelped like the Dog. *I'll get you for this, Dad*, she thought darkly.

People next to her started edging a bit further away.

"Do it again," said Dad, feeling the Dog wriggle and fearing he was going to yelp again. "Loud as you like."

"Yowp yowp yelp!" Nat yelped again. People were now pointing and moving away from her like she carried the plague.

"Barmy, you two, barmy," said Mick. "The Froggies deserve you, they really do. Pull over at the first big lay-by when you get off the ferry and I'll show you what car a REAL driver drives. I'll give you a clue. It's brilliant. It's much better than yours."

He moved off, pushing people out of the way. Nat was about to kick Dad really hard when she realised Darius had disappeared AGAIN.

"He'll have gone down to hide in the van," said Dad. "He's just keeping out of the way. He's not as daft as everyone at your school thinks he is."

But Darius was not in the van.

"Are you sure, love?" said Dad nervously as the ferry doors opened. All the cars were revving their engines, drivers eager to get their holiday started. "He is very good at hiding."

Nat chucked stuff about frantically. "He's not THAT good, Dad," she said. "I've been through everything." By now cars were beginning to roll off the ferry. People behind Dad started beeping their horns. "You're holding everyone up," said Nat.

"We can't go without him. Keep looking."

"HE'S NOT HERE. I CAN'T MAKE IT ANY CLEARER!" yelled Nat, emerging from a pile of clothes after tipping out all their suitcases. "And now I'M the one with pants on my head. Brilliant."

Dad sighed. "Right," he said, "we'd better go then. I'll have to tell the people in uniforms what's happened."

Their trip really *was* over now. Dad drove them off the ferry and up to passport control in silence, but just before he got there Nat started hopping about in the back of the van.

"Look!" mumbled Nat frantically. She was trying to point without anyone else seeing.

"What?" said Dad.

"Over there," she hissed. "I can see him."

But all Dad could see was Suspicious Mick driving away in a flashy but ugly black car. He was waved through the border by his colleagues, without even having to pause.

Suddenly Dad saw too.

"Brilliant," he said, chuckling, and drove on into France.

Suspicious Mick was waiting for them in his horrible car in the lay-by, as he said he would be. Dad pulled up next to him and got out. Mick began showing off his pride and joy. "I've spent thousands doing this up," he boasted. He was so happy showing off that he didn't notice Darius slide out from the back seat where he'd been hiding.

"Why didn't you tell me what you were doing?" said Nat, throttling him in the back of the van.

"I can't – *ack* – talk with your – *gak* – hands round my neck," squawked Darius.

"Too bad," said Nat. "I'd rather strangle you than get the answer."

Darius wriggled free. "You're too honest. You're really bad at telling fibs," he said. "If you

knew where I was hiding, you'd have given me away."

Eventually Suspicious Mick sped off into the distance, showing them all just how fast his horrible car could go, and they all breathed a sigh of relief. Nat was already worn out with worry. She reckoned she needed a lie-down in a dark room for about six weeks to recover. And they'd only just arrived in France!

"Righto," said Dad, folding up the map and sniffing the French air excitedly. "This is where the adventure starts!"

Five hundred metres and five minutes into the start of the adventure, the van broke down.

CHAPTER EIGHT

••••

"**Z**IS VAN EES A BLOCK OF – 'OW YOU SAY...?" THE French mechanic scratched his oily head with oily fingers. "A block of poo!"

"That's not right," said Nat. "You could call it a *pile*, a *bag* or even a *lump* of poo, but not a block."

Dad frowned. "So anyway," said Dad, to the mechanic, "what do you suggest?"

They were standing in a large, hot, smelly garage. The Atomic Dustbin was up on a ramp. Bits of engine lay scattered on the concrete floor. It looked like the van had eaten a scrapyard and then been sick.

"I suggest zis," said the mechanic. He made smashing noises and mimed a huge crusher. "I will give you ten euros for scrap."

"If you put Dad in it at the same time I'll pay YOU!" said Nat. She was hot and hungry and really annoyed.

"He can't scrap it – we've got to sleep in it!" said Dad.

"I weel try to repair if you insist. I will park it at ze back of ze garage while eet is getting ze fixing. Zere is a space between ze broken-down dustbin lorry and ze portable toilet. You can stay – no charge," said the mechanic generously.

"There you go, love," said Dad, "sounds perfect."

Nat slumped on the oily floor in a miserable heap.

"It sounds horrible," she said. "And besides, we haven't got time! We need to get to the house and start fixing it up before Posh Barry and Even Posher Linda and *stupid* Mimsy arrive, or Mimsy will blog about it and everyone back home will think you're utterly and totally useless and do you know HOW BAD THAT MAKES ME LOOK?"

"It doesn't make ME look too great either," mumbled Dad.

"There you go, thinking about yourself again," said Nat.

The mechanic, who had three children sulking at home, could see what was brewing – a full-blown family argument. He didn't want one here in his garage; he knew he would get one at home later.

"Look, stop ze fighting," he said, raising his voice over the noise of a tractor engine being disembowelled. "I do not like ze fighting. I only come to work in zis garage to get ze peace and quiet."

Nat ignored him. She was on a roll. "So now we're homeless, Dad, you big idiot. Mum always said if she left it to you we'd be homeless in six months."

Dad coughed and said, hopefully, to the

mechanic: "I don't suppose you can understand what she's saying, can you?"

"*Au contraire*," said the mechanic, "I understand perfectly. You are ze big idiot who has made ze little girl homeless."

He made a grand gesture. "I will 'elp," he said, "as long as your pet monkey puts down all ze tools." Darius, now covered in grease, put them down.

The mechanic went over to the ramp where the Atomic Dustbin squatted. "Eet is VERY dangerooos in 'ere, when you don't know what you're doing," he said.

"The piston rings are worn, the carburettor is split, the gasket's broke, and the big end's up the spout," said Darius. "The rack and pinion's gone, the front axle needs replacing and the brake linings are wrecked."

There was a pause. The mechanic glared at him. "Lucky guess," he said.

"Also, your ramp is broken," said Darius.

This was too much for the mechanic.

"Eeet is one thing to bring to me ze world's worst van, it is anozzer to argue and complain and make my ears bleed, but zere is NUZZINK wrong with my ramp," he said, hitting the button which makes the ramp go up and down.

Suddenly there was a horrible grinding noise. One side of the ramp gave way and the Atomic Dustbin slid right off it, landing with a huge crash, nose-first.

There was a horrible silence. The front end of the old camper van was totally mangled. It was ten times worse than before.

"It's very French in here," said Dad cheerfully, as the waitress slammed down his third coffee on the shiny, silver table in front of him with a rude scowl. They were waiting in a small café round the corner while the mechanic – who had had quite enough of them – was seeing if the van could be saved.

"Duh," said Nat, "we are in France."

Although, she thought to herself, *we won't*

be for long. She munched her (delicious) pastry happily. *I'll get a box of these for the journey home*, she decided.

She was in a good mood; SURELY they would have to go home now. And the best bit was – it wasn't Dad who'd smashed the van. So it wasn't his fault they couldn't get to the house, so he wouldn't be publically revealed as *a big useless idiot* after all.

Nat was going to call Penny Posnitch and go shopping as soon as she got back, she decided.

Darius glugged down a cup of thick black liquid.

"Are you sure it's OK to give Darius coffee, Dad?" asked Nat.

"Good point," said Dad. "It's probably not, on the whole." They watched as Darius fidgeted even more than usual in his seat. "It's like he's got new batteries," said Dad.

Just then the mechanic joined them. "I have ze bad news and ze good news," he said.

"What's the good news?" asked Dad.

"What's the bad news?" asked Nat.

"Ze bad news is my eldest daughter, she got a tattoo."

"That's not bad news," said Nat.

"Eet is bad news for 'er. She is grounded for two years."

"What's the tattoo?" said twitchy Darius, sounding genuinely interested. "Skulls, knives, a fire-breathing dragon?"

"It ees the name of ze stupid English band. Ze dirty grandmother, or something. I would like to meet zem."

There was a silence. Even Darius kept quiet. But Nat just KNEW that Dad would have to say something. She started kicking him but it was too late...

"I can introduce you," said Dad helpfully.

Nat grabbed him. "SHUT UP," she whispered loudly. But he burbled on.

"My Filthy Granny, they're called. Nice lads, when you get to know them."

"You know zem...?" asked the mechanic, astonished.

"I've played with them," said Dad modestly.

Nat was in a complete panic. She was kicking Dad REALLY HARD now. But he just leaned towards her and murmured, "Shush, I'm trying to get a connection between us. He might knock a few euros off the bill."

The mechanic picked up a heavy steering lock from his toolkit. "I want to meet zem so I can tear zeir 'eads off and shove zem in an exhaust pipe."

Even Dad now realised his mistake. "Ah, well, hang on a minute, when I say I KNOW them…"

The mechanic stood up and started hopping about. "For ze last year my 'ouse has been ze disco rave party with ze rock music of the feelthy grannies at full noise settings. I do not sleep becawse I can 'ear zem all the time with ze 'orrible guitars and the drums, always the drums. But now zis tattoo on my leetle princess. I cannot bear it."

He walked towards Dad, who was backing away from him in his chair. "And you KNOW ze Grannies?"

"*Grannies*, you say?" said Dad quickly. "Oh

no. I thought you said, er, em, um…"

"Bunnies!" said Nat. "Dad was in a band called My Filthy Bunny. And they were rubbish. Come on, does he look like a rock star?"

Dad looked offended but the mechanic took a deep breath, looked at Dad hard, and then started to laugh. "I see you are right," he said, chortling. "Your father 'e is ze old man with ze bald patch and ze beer belly and ze bad clothing."

"So's Elton John," muttered Dad sulkily.

"What's the good news?" said Nat, desperately changing the subject.

"Can I have a glass of cognac?" said Darius, looking at the drinks on offer.

"Yeah, course," said Dad, not really listening.

"No!" said Nat. "It's booze!"

"I can fix ze van in one week," he began. Dad groaned. "Can you stay in ze 'otel to wait, or are you too poor?"

"We're not poor," said Nat defensively.

The mechanic patted Nat on the shoulder. "Your father, 'e looks poor."

"That's what mum says," said Nat. "Dad, you're now embarrassing me in TWO countries; well done. I told you not to dress like a hobo."

"I'm smart casual," said Dad, sounding hurt.

"You got those T-shirt and jeans from the charity shop next to school, which I've told you not to go in because my friends can see you in there, and that jacket's from a bin."

"It is not from a bin," said Dad. "I found it on a bus."

"Your ramp broke the van, so you should pay for the hotel," said Darius simply.

"I hadn't thought of that," said Dad, "but I suppose he's right."

The mechanic glared. The Dog tried to lick something sticky off Darius's hand.

There was a stand-off. But then…

The mechanic suddenly straightened, with a big smile on his face. "I can do better than that!" he said. He took out a photograph from his wallet.

"How's that man going to help us?" said Dad, looking at the picture.

The mechanic snatched it back, offended. "Wrong photo," he said. "And zat is no man, it is my wife!"

"Sorry, don't have my glasses on," said Dad hurriedly.

Nat tried to hide under the table.

The mechanic took out another photo. This time it was of a big blue and white barge, sailing down a pretty little tree-lined canal.

"You will stay on *La Poubelle*," he announced grandly. "For free."

Oh no, thought Nat, *Dad's heard the magic word – free.*

"Tell me more," said Dad.

CHAPTER NINE

• • • •

I T SEEMED VERY SIMPLE.

The mechanic's cousin had recently bought this barge off the internet after enjoying too many cognacs and hadn't had time to move it to a canal near him. As luck would have it, though, he lived quite near to Posh Barry's haunted wreck.

The mechanic said his cousin had wanted to move the barge himself, but it was very slow and he couldn't get the time off work.

"See what happens when you have a proper job," said Dad to Nat, sounding pleased.

Yeah, you can afford to buy a boat, thought Nat.

"It is ze perfect plan, no?" said the mechanic. "You sail ze barge down to 'im while I mend ze block of poo. Zen I drive ze mended poo van to you at ze end."

Then he looked at Darius, adding: "And you don't write ze horrible things about my garage on ze online web, deal?"

Just then, Dad did something extraordinary. He looked Nat straight in the face and said:

"Darling girl, I know this isn't the holiday you wanted. If you want to go home now, we can. I'll just tell Posh Barry that I can't mend his house after all. It's OK, no one thinks I can do it anyway."

At that moment, Nat felt really sorry for him. And she knew she wanted him to prove everyone wrong. He could do it. He was flipping well going to.

Besides, they were going on a luxury barge, with proper beds and a living room and an inside loo and everything. It sounded WAY better than camping out in the Atomic Dustbin.

"Let's do it, Dad," she said, wondering if she was making a MASSIVE MISTAKE. Dad jumped up and offered her a high five.

"Don't leave me hanging," he laughed as Nat just eyed him suspiciously.

Eventually she relented and gave him the high five. She was starting to regret this already.

According to the mechanic, the barge was "eezy-peezy" to drive.

"She has ze engine and ze wheel of steering. Even ze chimpanzee could drive 'er," he said.

"See?" said Nat, nudging Darius, who was tipping little packets of sugar into his mouth, "Even you could do it, chimpy."

Dad sat back in his chair contentedly. Even Nat started to relax. She was going on a CRUISE. Like posh people do. Flora Marling, the goddess of class 7H, and the most popular, beautiful and awesome girl EVER, went on a cruise once. She was so awesome she said it was: "like, really lame".

In her head, Nat was starting to practise that phrase for when she got back.

Then Dad said the terrifying words: "It sounds almost too good to be true."

Nat suddenly felt sick.

Other things that Dad had said sounded 'almost too good to be true' over the years included:

1. The time he had DEFINITELY WON his OWN WEIGHT IN DIAMONDS! If he just agreed to buy a lifetime's worth of *Knitting World* magazines. He was still waiting for the diamonds, but on the plus side he now owned his own weight in sensible knitwear patterns.

2. The time Dad sent off for an expensive mystery cure for his Bald Spot Which Must Never Be Named, which was GUARANTEED TO WORK!!!!! It did work – he got sent a hat.

3. The time he tried to make some extra money by buying real antiques from car boot sales. Dad reckoned there were lots of people who were too daft to know what things were really worth. He

was right – *he* was too daft to know what things were really worth. He bought a 'Picasso' painting that was actually done by a cat ("To be fair, the cat *was* called Picasso," said Dad just before Mum hit him with it), a bed slept in by Henry the Eighth with 'made in Taiwan' stamped on the bottom, and a hoard of golden pirate coins that were not so much *pieces of eight* as *bits of plastic*. When he came home with Excalibur, though, Mum finally put her foot down and chased him round the kitchen with the rusty old sword till he promised to never buy an 'antique' again.

Nat tried to tell herself to stop worrying. *Maybe THIS TIME things will be different*, she thought. *Just maybe…*

Soon the mechanic was back in the café, with maps, keys, three life jackets and a compass. Dad LOVED maps, which was odd because he could get lost crossing the road.

"So what's this thin blue line?" asked Dad, making Nat cringe.

"It is ze canal. Ze canal zat ze boat goes on,"

said the mechanic, looking worried. "Blue means water. You have seen a map before, no?"

The blue line snaked through the map. "You start here," said the mechanic, spreading the map on the crumby café table and pointing to a spot on the blue snake.

"That would be north by north-east of here," said Dad wisely, staring at the compass like he knew what he was doing. "No, due south," said the mechanic, turning the compass round.

"You are going to pay attention, aren't you, Dad?" said Nat. "We don't want to end up on the Isle of Wight. Like that time you were supposed to be taking me to Alton Towers."

"We had a nice time on the Isle of Wight," said Dad defensively. "Plus, it gave you more of a surprise."

"Don't pretend you did it on purpose," she said. "You thought we were there. You thought the Isle of Wight ferry was one of the rides."

"Small misunderstanding," said Dad.

"Small? You had a stand-up row with the ticket

man, got us banned from the ferry for life and had to pay a fisherman to take us back."

"Kids, eh?" said Dad, smiling at the mechanic.

Soon they had loaded all their things and the Dog on to the mechanic's speedy little truck and were off to see *La Poubelle*. It was quite a drive to the boat so they took the motorway, which was almost empty of traffic.

Nat was enjoying the fact that it would have been much busier if they'd taken their slow old van, due to the queues of traffic it always caused. It was a treat not to have other drivers shout rude things at them.

Eventually they pulled off on to a series of ever smaller roads, bordered by tall slim trees, each road prettier than the last. They were getting deeper into the heart of the countryside and Nat was finding it hard to stay grumpy.

It was another beautiful summer afternoon. The sunlight shone through the trees and sparkled all around them. Birds sang and crickets chirped.

Nat daydreamed about long hot days sunbathing on deck, getting an amazing tan and stuffing her face with cake. She knew she should be full of dread and fear, bearing in mind she was with both Dad AND Darius, but she couldn't help being cheerful. This boat trip actually sounded brilliant. Maybe, just *maybe* Dad had done something right this time.

And then she saw the boat.

CHAPTER TEN

• • • •

I SHOULD HAVE KNOWN, SHE THOUGHT MISERABLY, AS she stared at the horrible boat. *I should have flipping well known.*

The barge looked nothing like the photograph. It was older and more battered than the pyramids, and frankly, thought Nat, the pyramids looked more likely to stay afloat.

It was huge and boxy, like those great big metal containers you see on cargo ships. It was like a caravan that had been pushed in a canal. One end was a bit pointier than the other and Nat guessed that was the front, but it was hard to tell. There was a little wooden wheelhouse towards the back end, with the steering wheel in.

There was no getting away from it – *La Poubelle*, sitting in a pool of its own grime, was ugly. Eyesight-manglingly ugly. Nat tried to find its good side. There wasn't one. Blue and white paint was peeling off every surface, it was covered in oil streaks and dents, the portholes were cracked and there were thick black tyres tied on the sides with fraying rope.

"Ze photo was taken a few years ago," admitted the mechanic.

"It doesn't look too bad with your eyes closed," joked Dad. Nat scowled at him.

They all clambered aboard, the mechanic heading for the wheelhouse to start her up.

Some people emerged from clean, shiny boats nearby and started laughing and pointing at them. Nat didn't know what they were saying but she thought she heard the words *idiot* and *Anglais*.

"What do you think they mean by *idiot*?" asked Dad.

"I want to ring Mum," said Nat, thoroughly fed up with being laughed at YET AGAIN. "I want to call her *right now*."

Dad shuffled about sheepishly as the mechanic unlocked the cabin doors. He fished out his mobile. "Probably best you just tell her all the *nice* things about the trip," he said. "We don't want to worry her."

Just gimme the phone, Baldy, thought Nat as she held out her hand.

Dad looked at his phone. "I've got a text from the phone company." He squinted at it. "Read that for me, love, would you?" he said. "I've put my glasses down somewhere."

Nat snatched the phone and read the message. "'Dear valued customer,'" she said, "'you have exceeded your roaming charges and—'"

"What are roaming charges?" asked Dad.

"It's the massive amounts of money they charge idiots who forget to turn off the internet on their phone when they go abroad!" shouted Darius.

Dad looked worried. "Carry on reading," he said.

Nat groaned, guessing he was one of those idiots. "It says 'We have cut off your phone until the bill is paid in full.' Then there's a massive number." Dad grabbed the phone off her. He stared at it in a sickly way for a few minutes then put it in his pocket.

"Have you got yours?" he asked hopefully, although he knew the answer.

Nat scowled at him. "No, Dad," she said, "you made me keep it at home because I couldn't be trusted not to run up MASSIVE BILLS, remember?"

"Oswald sold mine," said Darius. "He did say he'd steal me another one for Christmas though."

"Oh, well, this'll be nice," Dad said, with a weak smile, as he loaded the barge with their things. "No phones, no emails. Be like an old-fashioned proper family holiday."

Then the air was ripped apart by a massive farty roar as the barge's engine coughed into life.

"Pardon me," joked Dad, rubbing his stomach. "French food." Darius laughed hysterically; Nat just sighed. *Boys*.

Thick black smoke was now pouring from a chimney sticking out of the wheelhouse. The whole boat shook and the Dog, who till now had been dozing in the car, began to howl. "It sounds like an air raid!" shouted Nat.

"Do not worry," the mechanic called out from the wheelhouse, "it just needs to warm up."

"Warm up *what*?" said Nat, watching the smoke swirl around the canal bank. "The polar ice caps? That thing is putting out so much pollution we're gonna melt them off the planet in a week."

"It's not so bad," said Dad. "In fact, it reminds me of the Atomic Dustbin. Don't you think?"

"Yes, Dad, it does, which is the worry. When our van breaks down we just get stuck at traffic lights, or block a roundabout for a couple of hours. If we break down in this, we get shipwrecked. Shipwrecked is worse, Dad, everyone knows that."

"Aaarrrr!" said Darius in his best pirate voice. "Tonight we'll be dinin' in Davy Jones's Locker!"

A beautiful wooden barge, decorated with yards of pretty ribbons, streamers and flowers glided gently by. On deck, a man and a woman in very smart clothes and with very snooty faces stared at the smoking barge.

"Oh, I say," said the man, who was English and wore a blue blazer with a crest on the pocket, "I do hope you're not thinking of going anywhere in that thing."

"No," said Nat.

"Yes," said Dad.

"Aaarrrr!" said Darius. "Get lost, you scurvy dogs."

"They must be those river gypsies we were warned about," said the woman, alarmed. "I've read about them in the papers. They're probably stealing that boat."

The man looked at Nat and Darius and pulled a face. "It's the children I feel sorry for," he shouted, over the noise of *La Poubelle*'s engine.

So do I, thought Nat, *so do I*.

It was almost time to cast off. The mechanic was just going over with Dad one last time how to start the engine and steer the boat. Dad was nodding and making "uh-huh" noises but Nat saw that he wasn't really listening. He had that look on his face that said: "I'm pretending to listen but really I'm thinking about pork pies or ukuleles or Christmas cracker jokes or how to get the highest score on my new phone app game."

Nat paid attention because she knew *someone* had to know how to drive the barge. Then she heard a flushing sound from inside the boat. The mechanic heard it too. He grabbed Dad urgently and took him inside the barge. "Now I must show you ze most important thing before I go," he said, rushing through the living room and opening a little wooden door to the loo.

"Oi," said Darius, who had only just finished doing what he was doing, "wait your turn."

The mechanic pulled him out and quickly lifted

up the big red lever that flushed the loo.

"After you make ze poo-poo, zis must always be UP," he said sternly. "Else the river water comes into ze boat and…" he made a downwards motion. "You have seen ze fillum *Titanic*, no?"

"Yeah," said Darius with relish, "only it won't be a floating iceberg that will sink us, it'll be a floating—"

"Yes, we get it," snapped Nat. She felt a creeping sense of doom. They were one flush away from disaster. She looked at Dad and Darius, who both had memories like old-age-pensioner goldfish, and knew she would spend the entire time panicking about the flipping loo. This was NOT the relaxing break she had been promised.

Now she was inside, and her eyes had got used to the gloom, Nat looked around the barge. It was almost as ugly on the inside as out. The portholes were grimy with green mould so it looked a bit like they were underwater already. There was a large but dingy living room with a table and a tatty sofa. The TV had a big crack in the glass.

"I've seen French telly," said Dad, looking at the screen. "It's so bad someone probably threw a brick at it."

"Shotgun this cabin," shouted Darius, who had chosen the biggest one, at the back. He was spread out on the bed, muddy shoes and all.

"You can't let him have that one, Dad," said Nat, who wanted it for herself.

"I don't mind," said soft Dad. "Go on, love, you choose next."

Nat looked around. She found a cabin that was dim and wooden-panelled. The light in here was greenish and the room smelt of mud. A pair of sad yellow curtains hung limply in front of a porthole, adding another unpleasant tinge to the colour scheme.

Nat thought the room looked like the inside of a stomach. But it was big and she tried to tell herself the bed looked comfortable.

Anyway, it was the least worst room, so she nabbed it.

Dad opened the door to his cabin, which was

as big and bright and inviting as a coffin. "Oh," he said, "well, I'll only be using it for sleeping."

The Dog ran in and lay full length on it. There was hardly any room at all now.

"Are we ready to go now, Dad?" said Nat.

"No," he said. "I have to go through all the stuff about the engine and steering and such." Nat buried her head in the pillow.

"We have done zat already," said the mechanic, who was beginning to have second thoughts about the whole thing.

"Oh yeah, silly me!" said Dad. "Slipped my mind."

What mind? thought Nat.

"Can I untie these ropes?" shouted Darius, who had gone back on deck.

"Nooooo!" shouted the mechanic, dashing up the stairs, with Dad and Nat behind him.

The boat was drifting away from the bank. "Turn ze wheel!" shouted the mechanic to Dad, trying to hop off. But now he had one foot on the bank, the other still on the barge.

"Righto," shouted Dad from the wheelhouse. The gap between the barge and the bank suddenly yawned wider.

"NO! Turn it *ze ozzer* way," yelled the mechanic, doing the splits.

But the gap was just too wide…

There was a loud splash.

"CENSORED – NOT FOR PUBLICATION. FOR ADULTS ONLY!" shouted the mechanic. He shouted more things but Nat missed them due to the laughter of the other boaters on the marina. She saw one man videoing everything. *Oh great, I'll be an internet star in about half an hour*, she thought. *Thanks again, Dad.*

"Sorry," shouted Dad, "see you in a week, bye!"

CHAPTER ELEVEN

• • • •

MEANWHILE, BACK HOME IN ENGLAND, SOMETHING terrible was happening. Something that, like a sneeze on top of a snowy mountain, seems harmless at first.

Unless you're at the bottom of the mountain watching the big avalanche that the sneeze has caused hurtle towards you and you wished some people would not climb mountains with a cold.

Bad News Nan was planning a surprise visit to France. *AAAAA- CHOOOOHH!*

Mum was the first to hear of this plan. She came

home at lunchtime with a splitting headache, only to find Bad News Nan in the kitchen, both hands in the biscuit tin.

"Mmmf," said Nan, mouth full of Hobnobs. "Youm blmmmf lmfff."

Mum knew her well enough to realise what she saying, even with biscuits IN and teeth OUT.

What she was saying was: "Have you heard the bad news about Mister Bartelski who runs the mini market?"

Mum opened the fridge, and stared unhappily at its white, *empty* interior. She nodded her head. She wasn't feeling very well and did NOT want to hear the bad news. "Yes, I heard," she fibbed. "I've heard all about it. Every little tiny detail. So you don't need to tell me."

But that didn't stop Nan. She liked this story and was going to tell it anyway. "Wfff Mishhtrr lumff blasgh…" she began, which meant:

"Well, Mister Bartelski was up a ladder and had a row with Mrs Perkins from the estate about the price of his doughnuts. You know Mrs Perkins, she's the one with the plastic hip and dirty kitchen surfaces. He got so angry, he fell off his ladder into the freezer compartment. Now he's in Accident and Emergency having a bag of sprouts and a hot dog sausage removed."

Mum didn't want to know where they were getting removed from. She was supposed to be at work, there was nothing to eat and she was missing Dad and Nat. Worse, for some reason she hadn't been able to get through to Dad's phone. She noticed a red letter from the mobile phone company, ripped it open and saw Dad's massive unpaid bill. He'd been cut off.

Great, she thought. *A perfect day. The only thing that could make it worse would be if Bad News Nan sits in the kitchen for the next hour, talking at me.*

Which is exactly what happened.

So Mum heard about:

Mrs Waddington's weeping warts,

Mr Dhaliwal's drooping dog,

Mrs Nimrod's nasty niece.

Bad News Nan loved an audience who weren't able to run away. She liked it so much she once volunteered to chat to those people in hospital who haven't got visitors. It saved the hospital thousands of pounds' worth of medicine because after she'd been, all those patients said they were better, and could they go home now, please, Doctor, quick, before she comes again?

Finally Mum made toast and scarpered into the living room. She turned the news channel on. But there was still no escape because Bad News Nan followed her and carried on talking over the TV. Mum started to get confused as to what was actually happening in the world and what was going on down the road. All the stories got jumbled up.

There was an earthquake in Japan that scratched Phyllis Glomm's new mobility scooter.

There were riots in the Middle East because of Mrs Barter's dirty net curtains.

And England won a very important football game because of a last-minute goal from next door's missing cat.

So it wasn't really Mum's fault that she wasn't listening when Bad News Nan said something that was *actually quite important*.

See, Bad News Nan liked a bargain. And she had found a nice cheap flight online. So she thought she might as well come and join them all in France.

So, she said, burbling on, could Mum let Dad and Nat know so they could pick her up from the airport?

"Yes," said Mum, who'd been saying "yes" nonstop all afternoon, though she had absolutely no idea what she was saying yes to any more.

CHAPTER TWELVE

••••

"SHIVER ME TIMBERS!" SHOUTED DAD, GRIPPING THE big wooden steering wheel and giving it a few trial turns. "Avast behind. Splice the mainsail and run up the, er, whatever it is you run up, Aaaarrr!"

"Aaaarrr!" said Darius, on deck, jabbing Nat with a stick like a sword. "I'll pickle your giblets and fly them like a flag!"

The next hour, floating serenely under a beautiful blue sky, dotted with feathery white clouds, should have been relaxing and lovely.

It wasn't.

Dad was rubbish at steering. He had no patience. It took the boat a long time to respond to the wheel, by which point Dad had panicked and tried to turn the other way. So they zigzagged drunkenly down the wide canal, narrowly missing boats, canoes and fishermen.

But NOT missing a heron's nest, which exploded in twigs as Dad ploughed straight through it. The heron flapped up from the destroyed nest and squawked angrily at Dad.

Then it flew over and pecked Nat on the back of the neck.

"Ah, ah geroff!" she screamed. "It's not *my* fault. Peck Dad!"

But the bird wasn't going anywhere. Nat ran in little circles, waving her arms frantically, getting nipped by the large fowl's sharp beak. The laughter from passers-by on the riverbank got louder.

"It won't eat you, it only likes fish!" yelled Darius unhelpfully.

"That's what you think!" shouted the flailing

Nat. "I think it wants a change of diet. Ow ow ow *that hurts*. Will you get it off me?"

"I probably shouldn't leave the wheelhouse," shouted Dad, leaving the wheelhouse. "I'm trying to avoid a sailing boat."

"Well get back in and avoid it!" replied Nat, still fighting off the bird. Over the flapping of wings and the squawking and the laughter, she heard the unmistakable sounds of panic from downriver and guessed it was the person on the other boat, seeing the barge heading steadily towards them.

"AAAAARRR!" yelled Darius, and charged at the heron, waving his stick over his head. "It's a fight you want, is it?" The heron took one look at Darius and decided it didn't want to peck him in case it caught something nasty, so settled for one last big peck of Nat's head and flapped off to start rebuilding its nest.

"Get back to the wheelhouse, Dad!" said Nat. "Hurry!"

The shouting from the other boat grew louder. Dad rushed back and grabbed the wheel. He spun it round and slowly, very slowly, the barge began to turn. But it looked like it might be too little, too late. Darius stood on top of the wheelhouse. "Prepare to be boarded!" he shouted in his best pirate voice.

"Watch out for my boat! It's *really* expensive and it's better than *your* boat!" yelled a voice Nat thought sounded familiar.

She watched as they drew even nearer.

There was a man on the little white boat and he was hopping about in fury and helplessness as *La Poubelle* bore down on him.

Nat felt hot and cold. She *did* recognise the man.

He wasn't looking at her, he was holding a long pole to try and push the boats apart but even Nat could see that would be hopeless. Their dirty old steel barge was just too big and heavy.

Closer, closer…

Nat turned away to avoid seeing the accident. Surely any second there would be a horrible smash and then the sounds of sinking?

But nothing happened. Finally she plucked up the courage to look. They were past the little boat. They must have missed by a centimetre.

"Missed by a mile!" fibbed Dad.

Nat turned to look at the little boat they had just avoided colliding with.

The man was shaking his fist. Their eyes met.

It was Suspicious Mick.

"Look at me!" shouted Darius, waving something above his head. "We got so close I snatched their flag! This is great."

Wrong, thought Nat, as she watched Suspicious Mick's eyes almost disappear in a deep frown. He took in Nat, Dad, Darius and the Dog. He stopped waving his fist and started stroking his chin.

This was not great. This was *awful*.

"You know, this really is ever so relaxing," shouted Dad from the wheelhouse a little while later. They were chugging along in the middle of the wide canal, watching fields and trees and little red-brick houses slip by. "I think we should have *all* our holidays on a boat from now on."

Dad was sitting on deck in a little canvas chair he'd found, and to Nat's alarm, DARIUS seemed to be steering. Dad was wearing a string vest because he'd read a magazine article which said string vests were very NOW, and it was so hot he'd put a little knotted hanky on his Bald Spot Which Must Not Be Named.

Nat thought Dad did not look very NOW. He looked very THEN.

She had seen fading photographs of her grandfather at the seaside, way before she was born, when Dad was a little boy. Her grandfather was wearing a string vest and a little knotted hanky too. *Everyone* who had seen the photo had laughed at him, even Dad.

And now it looked like Nat was sailing through France with that man from the photo, giving everyone that saw him a good chuckle.

So no, Nat was not *ever so relaxed*. She should have been; she was on a sort of cruise, on a properly beautiful canal, on a genuinely lovely sunny day.

But in fact, she was *ever so* very tense. She had way too much to worry about. She had even come up with a MASSIVE list of things she should be worrying about.

NAT'S LIST OF THINGS TO WORRY ABOUT:

1. Dad was letting Darius steer the barge. This was clearly INSANE. When she had pointed this out to him – with only a little bit of shouting – Dad had argued that Darius was so fidgety that it was safer to keep him busy. Nat was sure Dad was just being lazy. (She heard a big slurp as Dad chugged down a massive glass of pop and flicked through his DIY book. *Yup*, she thought, *lazy lazy lazy.*)

2. Suspicious Mick had seen her. Worse, he had seen Darius and the Dog. They were not supposed to be in France. Nat had seen a war film where people who were not supposed to be in France got shot. OK, those people were spies, but it was still a worry.

3. If they ever DID get to Posh Barry's stupid, falling-down house, bodger Dad was going to kill himself to death putting his fingers in a socket, or sawing his own leg off.

4. She had to do LOO WATCH twenty-four hours a day, at least.

5. She needed to make ANOTHER list just to cover all the normal embarrassing things Dad was obviously going to do, not to mention Darius!

"I've come up with an idea to make us a fortune so we can spend all our time doing this," Dad said, sucking thoughtfully on his pen. He'd managed to chew the top off and his teeth had gone inky black. "I'm going to write a book about giving up our busy life in England—"

"Busy?" laughed Nat. "OUR busy life? *Mum's* busy, and *I'm* busy, but *you're* not."

"I'm going to write the true story of how we gave it all up to live the free and easy life on the canals. I just need a title to get me started."

There was a horrible shrieking noise from the front of the boat, and a whoop of laughter from Darius. A cloud of white feathers shot up over the wheelhouse.

"Ah yes," said Dad, "that's it. *Sailing Over Swans*."

"We've been on the canals for about two hours, Dad," said Nat. "You're not going to get much of a book out of that."

"I might have to pad it out a bit," Dad admitted, "and use my imagination, but everyone does that. You don't think travel writers actually go to all those places, do you?"

"Yes, I think they all do. I think that's the point."

She could tell Dad wasn't really convinced. He went back to scribbling and pen sucking and teeth blackening. Nat hated it when Dad tried to write a book. It happened every so often, usually when Mum shoved a bunch of red bills under his nose and asked him where he thought the money was coming from.

Dad would put on his red velvet jacket and spend the next week staring out of the window holding a pen. She could never bring her friends home when Dad was trying to write because he spoke to them in a writer-y way.

Penny Posnitch hadn't been round since Dad told her that her 'dark tresses cascaded down her back like a flock of elks down a mountain'.

"He was just being poetic," explained Nat with a sigh.

"I don't care," said Penny. "I spent ages blow-drying my hair, and anyway, elks don't flock."

Finally Dad would print out a few chapters and send them off to publishers. Then he would sit around reading car magazines, deciding which sports car to buy after he'd become a massive bestselling author.

A few weeks later, he'd get the usual reply that would basically say: STOP WASTING OUR TIME, LOSER. The car magazines got chucked in the bin and Dad would go back to writing Christmas cracker jokes and hiding the red bills under the cushions.

Nat went and sat with her feet dangling over the side of the barge for a while, watching the ripples in the water. She told herself she had far too much to worry about to enjoy herself. But she WAS in grave danger of enjoying herself, she admitted reluctantly.

She munched on a rather lovely cheese baguette Dad had bought from the café that morning that she had to admit tasted OK. She sat with Dad for a while, looking at little white farms in the distance, or the flowing rows of green grapes, and ignoring the revolting sounds of Darius practising his long-distance spitting.

Finally the sun began to go down. Nat lay on a long cushion on the deck and stretched out. She heard the pop of a cork as Dad opened a bottle of wine. The Dog padded over and curled up next to her. Despite all the stuff she had to worry about, her eyelids grew heavy, and she began to drift off into a deep relaxing sl—

Nat came round to the sound of a loud bang.

"Who put that sandbank there?" shouted Darius.

"Hueeerk," said Dad, who was hanging over the side, losing his baguette. "Sun and wine and boats make me feel a bit... bleeeark."

Nat sighed.

By the time Dad had recovered it was dusk. The barge seemed to have come to a standstill, so they decided to stay for the night.

CHAPTER THIRTEEN

••••

NAT WOKE EARLY, WITH MISTY PALE LIGHT SLICING through the yellow curtains in her little cabin. She lay there, confused for a second, wondering where she was. There was birdsong everywhere and she had a lovely floating feeling. Sleepily, she opened her curtains.

The canal was steamy and magical in the young light. She saw a row of ducks and then even a shimmering kingfisher, so close she could have almost touched him. She followed him with her eyes, entranced, right up until the moment she saw Darius *weeing in the canal.*

She shut the curtains and put the quilt over her head.

She was woken for the second time by Dad frying bacon. The three of them munched their breakfast on deck, watching the world go by. They were still stuck on the sandbank but no one felt like trying to start the horrible engine.

Finally, Dad said the dreaded words: "Righto, I suppose we should get going then."

"Can we wait until no one's looking?" said Nat.

"It's getting busier," said Dad, "so the sooner we try the better."

There is a thing called 'beginner's luck', which Nat thought was the only explanation for the way they slipped off the sandbank, with no fuss. Only one man in a canoe was overturned. Nat thought that was a bit of a triumph.

In fact, they pootled slowly down the slow, wide canal all morning and NOTHING TERRIBLE happened. Nat knew it just meant Dad was saving up for a big one.

She was right.

By the afternoon the canal was surprisingly busy. There were many more boats of varying shapes and sizes. There were long slender wooden barges painted blues and greens, decorated with buckets of flowers. There were large pointy plastic-white boats, sailing boats with high elegant sails, and fat little chugging boats that rolled and bobbed through the water.

They all have one thing in common, thought Nat. *NOT ONE is more ugly than ours. Dad, you've done it again*.

A few people to waved at *La Poubelle*, while most looked at the barge with alarm. Nat pulled her big floppy sunhat down over her face.

"We must be coming up to a big town," said Dad. He peered at the map. "We're either here –" he pointed to a town – "or possibly this different town here..."

They were coming into the sort of large town that guidebooks and articles in posh magazines bang on about endlessly. 'Oooh, it's very *authentic*,' they say, which just means 'real', but means it in a posher way.

Nat knew that other words to watch out for in guidebooks included:

HISTORIC, which means: 'Boring – avoid unless you want to be dragged around a toothbrush museum, cold church or (aaaargh!) *ancient ruins*.

LIVELY, which means: 'Full of drunks and so noisy you'll need to shove your head in the wardrobe to get some sleep.'

TRANQUIL, which means: 'Dead – up a mountain with only a goat for company.'

On the other hand:

DISAGREEABLE, NOTHING HERE WORTH A VISIT, means: 'Normal – proper shopping centre, cinemas, possibly even arcades and definitely plenty of delicious fried chicken takeaways. Go go go.'

However, a proper guidebook would at least have told Nat that tonight, in the town they were heading for, was the River Regatta.

The River Regatta was basically a floating fun fair, parade, boat race and huge party all in one. Tourists loved it and the tourist officer who had come up with the idea had been elected deputy mayor.

Everyone is welcome! said the posters on the walls and billboards they sailed past. Of course, Nat couldn't ask Dad what they meant because he couldn't read French, even though he pretended he could. They might just as easily be saying:

Stop and turn around! Massive waterfalls/sea serpents/whirlpools of doom coming up – if you're very lucky you might get away with only being lightly killed!

They followed the canal right through the centre of the town. High brick walls loomed either side of them. Nat could hear cars and people and music coming from behind the walls. Boats were moored on little platforms on both sides of the canal. Dad slowed the engine right down. And then, ahead of them, two massive lock gates, like doors to a giant's castle, blocked the way. Dad looked nervous.

"What do we do now?" said Nat.

"Food," said Darius, sniffing the air. Nat realised she was ravenous. A lovely cooking smell drifted towards them. "Let's park."

"Genius idea," said Nat. "Um, Dad… you do *know* how to park, don't you?" she asked.

Dad shifted uncomfortably in the wheelhouse and gave the wheel a turn experimentally. "I don't suppose it's much different from parking a car," he said.

"You're hopeless at parking a car," said Nat.

"Reverse into a parking space, that's what Oswald says when he's driving My Filthy Granny's van," said Darius, and pulled the lever to slam the engine into reverse. The water churned behind the barge and it began moving backwards, slowly at first, then with gathering speed.

Nat looked at Darius in alarm. "I NEED pizza," he explained. "Or fried chicken. Or fried chicken pizza."

Nat drooled at the thought. "Yeah, you're

right," she said. "Hurry up, Dad. Darius will be putting the Dog between two slices of bread soon." The Dog slunk down the stairs into the cabin.

"Find me a parking space then," said Dad, grabbing the wheel. "It must be easier than parking at the supermarket. I can't bash anyone's headlights out."

"No, but you could sink a load of boats," said Nat, as Dad missed a little white yacht by centimetres.

"Why did you say that?" said Dad. "I'd just got my confidence up."

"Left a bit, Dad," shouted Nat. Dad swung the wheel. The boat went right. "The *other* left," shouted Nat, before spotting an empty platform. "There's a space. I think you just kind of slowly crash into it and then tie it up."

"Crashing's easy," said Dad. "So you do the crashing and I'll do the tying up. I'm good at knots. I got a Scout badge." Nat got into the wheelhouse nervously. "You sure, Dad?" she asked.

"Yeah, just take the wheel. When I say brake, put the brake on."

Nat looked around. There was a wheel, a couple of broken dials and a gear lever. Nothing looked like a brake.

"Where's the brake?" she asked, voice rising in panic. "Dad, *the brake*?"

"I don't remember anyone mentioning a brake," said Dad.

"There isn't a brake on a boat," Darius said.

"Oh," said Dad, "how do we stop then?"

"If we slam the engine forwards, it will stop us going backwards," said Darius.

"Brilliant!" said Dad, hopping into the wheelhouse. "Let's do that."

"But then we'll be going forwards," said Nat.

"One problem at a time," said Dad. "We'll cross that bridge when we come to it."

"A *bridge too*?" wailed Nat. "It gets worse."

"It's just a *saying*," said Dad, slamming the engine forwards and not even remotely looking where he was going. "A saying like 'too many cooks spoil the broth', or 'a stitch in time saves nine', or..."

"Watch my boat, you damn fool!" shouted a voice.

"Dunno that one," said Dad, just before the crash.

CHAPTER FOURTEEN

••••

ALL CRASHES ON BOATS SEEM TO HAPPEN IN SLOW motion. *Which just means you get longer to panic*, thought Nat, over the shouting.

Their ugly old barge had backed into a handsome wooden vessel. A very energetic middle-aged man on the nice boat under attack was pushing *La Poubelle* off his paintwork with a large pole. Dad, on the other hand, seemed determined to sink him. "I'm not ENTIRELY sure I know what I'm doing," said Dad, whirling the wheel one way and then the other.

"Well, do something DIFFERENT!" shouted Nat.

"Hold tight," said Dad decisively. "I'm going to try something."

"Closing your eyes and hoping for the best does not count as trying something," said Nat, hunting for lifejackets.

And then something amazing happened. *La Poubelle* stopped crashing, moved forward and slid perfectly on to a large floating mooring. Nat looked at Dad. She was about to say, "I take it all back, you're obviously really good at this," when she noticed that, yes, he did actually have his eyes closed.

He opened them and looked around in surprise, then pretending he wasn't at all surprised, hopped on to the pontoon and began tying the boat up. He heard a heavy boot land on the pontoon behind him. He turned. It was the English man from the other barge. He was a big man, with thick grey hair like steel wool. Nat thought he looked like a TV ad for vitamins. Before Dad could say anything, the man offered him his large strong hand.

"I have to thank you," said the stranger. "That was the finest piece of seamanship I've seen for a long time."

Nat breathed a sigh of relief that there wasn't going to be another massive Dad row. But at the same time felt a tiny bit disappointed. She had *almost* been looking forward to Dad getting hurled off the pontoon. *I am so very wicked*, she thought.

Dad seemed to have been expecting to get chucked in the canal too, and looked surprised to find himself shaking hands. The English man was older than Dad, with hands like blocks of wood, covered in sandpaper. His face was leathery brown and lined like an old door left out in the rain, and covered with grey stubble. Bright green eyes poked out from under bushy eyebrows. Nat thought she heard Dad's fingers crack under the pressure of the handshake.

"I thought you were an incompetent moron who hadn't got the first clue about sailing and should be hung upside down in a bucket of boiling tar," said the man.

That's about it, thought Nat.

"Boiling sick's better!" shouted Darius.

The man laughed. "Absolutely right. He's a fine boy," he roared. "I bet you're a terror, right? Boy after my own heart!"

Oh, this just gets better, thought Nat sourly, watching Darius puff himself up. 'Fine' wasn't one of the words people usually said about Darius.

"But then I realised that you must have seen we'd just lost our rudder," continued the man. "You pushed us over to safety and then moored this thing like Admiral Nelson himself. I just wanted to shake your hand."

A very beautiful young woman joined them on the pontoon and the man released Dad and put his arm round her. "I should introduce you," he said. "I'm Rocky, and this is Emily."

"Ahhh," said Dad with a smile, "*I'm* sailing with my daughter too," said Dad.

"I'm not his daughter," said Emily, "I'm his wife!"

Nat went red. *You're getting chucked in the canal now, Dad*, she thought. But Rocky was just laughing, a deep and rather frightening sound.

"Everyone thinks that, don't worry," said Emily sweetly.

"Now, I insist on buying you all dinner!" boomed the man. "I won't take no for an answer."

Dad's not going to say no, thought Nat. *Free food? Try stopping him.*

"…And so there I was, several thousand feet up Mount Ummagumma, leg stuck fast in a crevasse, right arm broken in six places, and I'd just realised that it was an ACTIVE volcano. It was about to blow." Rocky was entertaining them with another action-packed story.

"Worse, my phone was just out of reach." He paused for dramatic effect. "Not that it would have done any good – I'd just been cut off because I'd forgotten to pay the phone bill!"

Everyone round the restaurant table laughed, except Nat, who had heard rather too much about

Rocky's adventuresome life.

"I'm sure Dad knows just how you feel," she said. Dad's phone was always getting cut off.

"Yes, I'm sure your father's been in all sorts of scrapes," said Rocky, meaning climbing active volcanoes looking for lost treasure. He punched Dad affectionately. Dad smiled but Nat knew he'd have a bruise on that shoulder for *ages*.

"How did you escape?" asked Darius, who had actually sat still for the whole meal. Rocky paused to drink a huge glass of wine in two gulps. He raised an eyebrow at a waiter who *hurried over with another bottle*.

ONE EYEBROW. Nat couldn't believe it. Dad couldn't summon a waiter with a car alarm and a huge flag that said: 'Please can you serve me, I'm starving.'

"Escape?" said Rocky. "Oh no, that's a whole other story. I don't want to get boring."

"Good idea, don't bother," said Nat, who thought Rocky was making her dad look even more useless than usual.

Everyone ignored her. She toyed with her crêpe sulkily. Apparently Rocky was an explorer, an adventurer, a travel writer, a pilot, sailor, engineer, poet, painter, deep-sea fisherman and concert pianist.

He had played polo with kings, hunted rhino in the Serengeti, and discovered a cure for warts.

And as far as Nat was concerned, he was also a big fat show-off.

How come you can do so much and Dad can do, well, not very much at all? she thought. But Dad wasn't feeling down about that, oh no. Just the opposite. Which was THE VERY WORST THING.

You see, Nat knew that Dad liked to fit in with whoever he was talking to. He was terrible with men in white vans. Instead of saying something normal like: "Good morning, Dave, lovely weather, sorry your wife's not been too well," Dad would say: "Orlright geez, today is sweet as, innit? Soz about the old ball and chain, what can you do, eh? Fierce," and other such gibberish.

A man in a van had once leaned out of his window and said to her: "Excuse me, young lady, but I think your father's having a seizure."

So of course tonight Dad had turned into Rocky. He was now ACTION HERO DAD. He didn't tell fibs, he just didn't tell the whole story.

Rocky would talk about hunting for food; Dad would say, oh yes, he'd done the same thing. The difference was, Rocky was talking about tracking down wild boar in Bolivia and Dad would mean tracking down wild boar *sausages* in the supermarket.

When Rocky and Dad both remembered watching the sun rise over ancient Inca ruins, Rocky had been there; Dad had watched it on a documentary.

Rocky went down the 'River of Certain Death' in the Himalayas in the shadow of Everest. Dad went down the 'Flume of Fun' at the local water park in the shadow of the burger van.

Hot-air ballooning? Rocky was swept a hundred miles across the skeleton coast of

Namibia, when he became tangled in the mooring ropes. Dad was dragged across a car park when he bought too many party balloons for Nat's birthday.

Nat spent the whole night terrified that Dad would be unmasked as A MASSIVE FRAUD. But she had an even bigger worry. With all Rocky's praise, she knew Dad was starting to believe he was actually a good sailor. This is just going to end horribly, she predicted…

…accurately.

Emily was staring affectionately at her husband. "Isn't he wonderful?" she gushed. "We only met a year ago. We kissed under the Eiffel Tower in Paris. I fell madly in love."

"Uuuuuurgh," said Darius, revolted. He put his fingers down his throat to improve the retch.

"Let me tell you about the first date I had with Nat's mum," said Dad. Nat kicked him under the table. "Shut up shut up shut up," she said.

Darius jumped off his chair. "Tell me," he said gleefully, watching Nat squirm. "We all want to know. Kissy kissy kissy."

"Shut UP, chimpy," said Nat, making a grab for him and knocking her plate flying. He ran off laughing and she chased him around the restaurant, weaving past waiters with trays of food held dangerously high above their heads.

"I think they will be friends forever," said soppy Emily, watching Nat chuck bread rolls at Darius's head. A waiter came over to Dad. "You must stop zis naughtiness."

"Oh, it's only a bit of harmless fun," said Rocky.

And then a waiter carrying a tray of hot fish soup tripped over Darius and they decided it was probably time to leave. Fast.

As he said goodnight, Rocky slapped Dad affectionately on the back, almost sending him into the canal. "Tomorrow I'm taking you around the town. Show you things tourists never see," he boomed.

Nat waited for Dad to turn Rocky down and tell him they had a long journey ahead and would need to get going in the morning, but he just smiled and said, "Sounds great!"

Nat's heart sank. Dad seemed to have forgotten they still had MILES to go to deliver the barge, and that they were still nowhere near even STARTING to fix up the Poshes' house. Nat couldn't let him get distracted. She could almost hear Mimsy laughing already.

She had to get them out of Rocky's clutches. But how?

CHAPTER FIFTEEN

. . . .

THE NEXT MORNING DAD HAD FORGOTTEN ALL ABOUT the house. He seemed super-content to just mooch about town with Rocky, who knew EVERYBODY, and was greeted like a long-lost friend wherever he went.

"Isn't it fantastic here?" said Dad to Nat, sitting on a bench in the market square, chugging hot chocolate.

There were stalls of ripe-smelling cheese, cured meats, sweet-smelling herbs tied with ribbon, glossy fruit and veg, and angry stallholders chasing Darius.

"Normally Darius would get chucked in the canal for taking all the sticky labels off that lady's jam jars," said Dad. They watched as the jam-jar lady saw Darius was with Rocky and ruffled the boy's untidy hair instead.

Later, after a long leisurely lunch and plenty more stories, Rocky gave them his guided tour around the town. He seemed to know about everything; from the clock tower to the bus stops.

Nat started to miss the 'Dad tour' of a town. Dad never knew anything about anywhere, so he'd just make it up. His tour would go something like:

"The wonky clock tower was a gift from King Ludwig the Unsteady in 1789. He thought it was straight. The town bus stops were built by the Romans. The first mayor was Dave the Flatulent and that's enough history, I think this café sells pork pies, let's try it. Oh, and don't tell Mum we went to the arcade again today— let's say we went to a toothbrush museum."

By now it was getting late. The town was busy and more boats were arriving all the time. "It's the last night of the festival," said Rocky. "You will not believe what happens on the canal tonight."

Do we get to put you in a sack with bricks and chuck you in? thought Nat. *I'd definitely buy tickets to see that.*

"Bring your boat round to the south marina by nine o'clock," said Rocky. "Look over the wall and you'll get a grandstand seat for something amazing. The lock is closed but I've spoken to my good friend Pascal the lock keeper…"

Of course you have, thought Nat. *Show-off.*

"…and he'll let you through. Remember, south marina, nine o'clock sharp."

"I can manage that," said Dad.

No, you can't, thought Nat.

"Of course you can," said Rocky, "a great sailor like yourself. Oh, you do have to be careful though because you reach three bridges and…"

"…I think I know what I'm doing," said Dad loftily.

"Sorry, Captain," Rocky said. "Of course you do; see you at nine."

"Dad, you *don't* know what you're doing," said Nat furiously, when Rocky and Emily had gone. "You don't even know what you're doing when you're at home doing things that you *should* know how to be doing."

"Have a bit more faith in me," said Dad. "Rocky thinks I'm a brilliant sailor."

"But, Dad, he's MASSIVELY WRONG," said Nat. She had tried to get hold of Mum with Emily's mobile but it had gone to the answer machine. She knew Mum could talk some sense into Dad, but she hadn't really wanted to leave a message that said:

"Mum, help, Dad thinks he's a cross between Admiral Nelson and Captain Jack Sparrow and we're all doomed so please DO SOMETHING."

So she'd just said:

"Hi, Mum, we're having a lovely time, missing you a lot. Wish you were here. I mean, I REALLY wish you were here."

"Come on," said Dad, "let's get in that barge and show this town exactly what we can do."

That's what I'm afraid of, thought Nat.

CHAPTER SIXTEEN

• • • •

THE BIG EVENT THAT NIGHT WAS THE HISTORIC RIVER Joust. It *wasn't* historic. It was dreamed up a few years ago by the new deputy mayor who wanted even more visitors to come to his town.

The supermarket car park was promptly turned into a spiffy new marina, and now every year, in honour of some made-up medieval battle, there was RIVER JOUSTING.

This was written on posters and leaflets everywhere. Written in French.

Along with a warning that boats should NOT

go into the north marina that night…

None of which could be read by the passengers on board *La Poubelle*.

The ugly old barge gave a great roar as its smoky old engine came to life once more.

Dad shouted, "Cast off, landlubbers!"

Nat (unwillingly) and Darius (eagerly) untied the ropes and the barge was soon weaving its way down the canal. It was fast becoming dark but there was just enough light to see the look of fear on other boaters' faces as the big rusty barge went by.

Nat noticed Darius had a tea towel round his head. "I'm a pirate," he said, waving a stick which he'd sharpened to a point with his little knife.

"You look like a rubbish shepherd in a school nativity play," said Nat, dodging out of the way of his jabbing stick.

They soon approached the big lock. The lock gates looked bigger and even more intimidating in the gloom. Dad slowed and waved to a man in a little hut. The man came out and waggled a warning finger at Dad.

"He wants us to go back," said Nat. "Do as he says, Dad."

But Dad wasn't just Dad. Tonight he was Captain Dad.

"Friend of Rocky," shouted Dad.

The lock keeper's face broke into a smile. "OK," he said, and began working the lock gates. They creaked open with a horrid grinding noise that sent the cowardly Dog scurrying back down into the cabins.

"This is a really bad idea, Dad," shouted Nat. "That's the noise you get when the doors to Dracula's castle open. It's never a good noise. Nothing fun happens when you start with that noise. You've seen the films."

"Landlubber," said Dad, pointing the boat into the lock. Around them were high walls, dark green with wet weeds. It was like they had sailed underwater. The lock-keeper's assistant ran down some slippery steps and grabbed their boat ropes, looping them around bollards.

"Think they're supposed to do that?" asked Dad.

"Why are you asking ME?" shouted Nat, properly scared. The huge gates in front of them began to open and thousands of gallons of water began frothing angrily towards them, spraying them all in the face. The noise of the churning water was tremendous.

"You've broken the lock and we're all going to die and then we'll be in massive trouble," wailed Nat.

The boat rocked from side to side as the water flooded in, raising them upwards. Dad smiled grimly at the lock keeper above him. He wasn't going to show fear, oh no. This was all in a day's work for Captain Dad.

"If we all get drowned, I'm telling Mum," shouted Nat. NOW Captain Dad looked nervous.

Eventually the boat was raised fully to its new height, the second set of lock gates in front of them opened and they were free to sail through into the new section of the canal. It was empty. It was quiet. It was spooky. Nat could see Captain Dad's brave face wasn't quite so brave any more. She didn't know if it was the threat of drowning or threat of Mum.

They sailed on regardless, until they approached a wide circular basin of dark water where they were faced with a choice of three bridges to go under: one leading straight ahead and one either side. Under the bridges and beyond there was only darkness. There was no obvious way to go.

"Maybe we should just park," said Nat.

"But Rocky's expecting us," said Dad. "We can't let him down."

"We don't know which way to go," said Nat. "Why didn't you just *listen* when Rocky was trying to tell you?"

"The town's over there," said Dad, pointing in the direction of lights, glinting off to the left. "We'll just go there."

"Where's the map?" said Nat.

"Map?" scoffed Dad. "Columbus didn't have a map and he found America."

"Yes, but he was looking for India," said Nat. "He was the most lost sailor in *the whole history of sailing*."

She could see Dad was wavering when Darius suddenly shouted: "Aaaarrr! Scurvy knaves."

He pointed with his jabbing stick and there, on the right-hand bridge, was the unmistakable figure of Suspicious Mick!

"In that case, we'd better go left!" said Dad, turning the wheel decisively.

And without knowing it, the barge and her doomed crew headed straight for the forbidden NORTH marina...

Meanwhile... The north marina was the newly created site of the un-historical River Joust. It was lit by flaming torches, flickering off the faces of the tipsy spectators. The joust was wildly popular with both locals and tourists with their lovely tourist euros – a simple contest powered by fake history and real wine.

The way it worked was simple: two beautiful,

delicate, slender wooden barges faced each other across the water. On the front of each barge was a raised platform. A contestant held a large wobbly pole like a lance. Then the two boats, propelled by teams of rowers, charged at one another.

The aim was to knock each other off the barge and a great boozy cheer would go up whenever anyone was tipped into the canal. This silliness went on until the wine ran out.

This year's competition was reaching a climax. Only two contestants had not been dunked. One was the great Rocky. As he stood on the platform, gripping his pole, he faced his opponent, a huge fat pastry chef no one had even managed to wobble, let alone tip into the water.

As he looked for a delicate area to shove his pole into, Rocky heard a coughing, grinding engine noise that sounded familiar. He decided he hadn't got time to worry about that now, he had a lardy chef to dunk. He gripped his pole and hoped his new friend the Captain was watching…

Sadly his new friend the Captain *wasn't* watching; he was in a dark tunnel, in trouble. It was HIS boat that was making the noise, and the noise was worse than usual. The engine was smoking madly. Thick black stuff was pouring out of the chimney with such speed and force that it had filled the whole tunnel, making them all cough and gasp for breath.

"Do something, Dad," spluttered Nat, dashing into the wheelhouse, "or we'll all be turned into kippers!"

"I've tried to cut the engine but the knob's rusted stuck!" shouted Dad over the roar. The engine was now getting faster, not slower. The boat began to pick up speed.

"Turn it the other way," yelled Nat.

"I did that," said Dad. "That's when it got stuck."

"You are an idiot!" shouted Nat.

"I know what I'm doing!" shouted back Dad.

Darius came running into the wheelhouse too. "The engine cannae take it, Captain!" he said.

"Ha, I've been dying to say that for ages."

Dad laughed.

"Except it's true," said Darius. "Which makes it way better."

"I'll fix it," said Dad. "Take the wheel, you two. Just keep going straight. You can't go wrong."

"Yes, we can," said Nat. "We can go ever so very much wrong. We're going wrong already. We went wrong when we left home and we've been going wronger every single day." She would have said more but she burst into another coughing fit.

"Rocky repaired his engine in a force ten off the coast of Cape Horn in a lee tide with a falling, er, something or other!" Dad reminded them.

"You do not know what any of that means!" yelled Nat. It really was noisy in the tunnel and they were going far too quickly. Behind them, white water splashed furiously.

"He fixed it with a bit of fishing wire and some chewing gum. I'm sure I can remember how." Dad held out his hand. "Darius, spit out your gum."

Dad dashed below with the sticky gum and

some wire and went into the room where the old engine lurked. It was big and hot and oily and vibrated like an electric jelly. He looked at all the moving parts.

"Rocky went into great detail about this engine, and it made perfect sense at the time," shouted Dad, before adding, "only now it makes no sense at all."

He concentrated. Without thinking, he popped the gum in his mouth.

"Is that your dad shouting?" asked Darius, who was steering with his eyes closed to see if he had any spider senses.

"What's he saying?" asked Nat, panicky.

"It sounds like 'aaagh uuuugh yuk'," said Darius.

"Will you open your eyes and look where you're going?" she shouted, grabbing the steering wheel.

"Gerroff!" he said, elbowing her sharply. "I'm in charge now."

They struggled and the wheel turned this way

and that. Dad came staggering in. "You're making me seasick," he said. "Gimme the wheel."

"No!" said Nat.

"No!" said Darius.

"Yes!" said Dad, grabbing the wheel and pulling hard. It came off in his hand. "That's not so good," he remarked. Then the boat shot out of the smoky tunnel like a shell from an old cannon.

Straight into the wrong marina – and headed right for the jousting barges.

CHAPTER SEVENTEEN

••••

"Oooooh," said the audience, who thought this was a new and interesting part of the joust. Some even applauded.

The former deputy mayor who, hot on the heels of his success with the River Regatta, had invented the River Joust and was promptly promoted to mayor, dropped his jaw and his wine glass at the same time.

What was going on? Where had the horrible barge come from?

This was terrible. Worse, he'd persuaded the

local TV news to cover the event. They had been looking a bit bored but now they perked up. "Get a close-up of that big ugly boat," said the reporter, "it's the most exciting thing to happen all day."

The cameraman stopped focusing on pretty girls in the crowd and swung his camera round to the action.

Rocky and the fat pastry chef were already moving towards each other for the final joust. But they were no longer looking straight ahead. Both men were staring in terror at the noisy, rusty, smoky, *out of control-y* barge chugging speedily towards them!

The rowers couldn't see Dad, but they did wonder what the horrible burning smell and grinding engine noises were. The brightest of them jumped overboard.

"Ah," said Dad, "we might be in the wrong place. And possibly at the wrong time."

"What have you done, Dad?" wailed Nat, horribly aware they were in a VERY wrong place at a VERY wrong time.

Nat took in all the faces staring down at her from the sides of the marina. People were cheering, or yelling, it was hard to tell. Flashguns were going off and she saw the horrible outline of a TV CAMERA.

"What in the name of heaven are you doing?" boomed Rocky, from his jousting platform. *La Poubelle* was less than twenty metres away now, and closing in fast. The noise from the crowd was tremendous but Rocky's powerful voice sliced through the cheering.

Dad rushed to the back of the barge, where there was a big rudder for steering. "It's all under control," he said. *La Poubelle* lurched hard to the right, heading straight for Rocky's wooden boat.

"Pretend we're part of the show," shouted Dad. "No one will know."

"*Zere is an out of control boat on ze canal zat is NOT part of ze show,*" shouted the Tannoy man VERY loudly through huge speakers.

"Ooops," said Dad.

The Tannoy boomed again. "*Get ready for ze*

crash. Ze crash is definitely coming, ze crash is defi— oh, it missed."

Missed, but only by centimetres. Nat was desperately tying on a grubby lifejacket to the Dog when out of the corner of her eye she saw Darius grab his jabbing stick. He was well within jabbing range of Rocky's backside. She wondered if he could resist it.

"Aaaaaghh, I've been stabbed amidships!" shouted Rocky, dropping his pole and toppling over. He hit the water with a huge splash and the crowd roared approval.

Nope, he couldn't resist it, thought Nat.

It's hard to swim when you're rubbing your bottom, and so it proved for Rocky, who thrashed about in the water, bobbing up and down.

"I'll save you!" shouted Dad, and ran about looking for a lifebelt. He grabbed something and threw it at Rocky. Unfortunately, it wasn't a lifebelt, it was the heavy wooden steering wheel Dad had pulled off earlier. The wheel hit Rocky squarely on the head. He went under like a stone.

"Brilliant, Dad," shouted Nat. "He was annoying, but you didn't have to kill him."

Rocky came up, spitting water. "Why are you doing this to me?" he spluttered.

"I win, I win!" shouted Jean-Jacques, the rotund pastry chef, who was the only jouster still standing. Unfortunately he was now in range of Darius's jabbing stick.

"Aaaarrgh!" yelled the Knight of the Cream Puff, following Rocky into the water.

"Serves you right," blubbled Rocky.

"I WIN!" shouted Darius, hopping about in delight. "I am King Pirate – everyone bow down and give me chocolate!"

With no one on the tiller, *La Poubelle* zig-zagged wildly across the marina. Then the inevitable happened – the smoking and clanging barge crashed heavily into the side of the prettiest, oldest and most delicate-est jousting boat, shivering all the timbers and making a big gash in the wooden hull, which water immediately began pouring in through.

"Sorry!" shouted Captain Dad, running back to the wheelhouse. "I think it's just dented." The painted boat began to sink. "You might want to plug that leak," he added helpfully.

"We're really ever so sorry," shouted Nat, trying to hide her face from the gaze of the onlookers, whizzing by in a horrible torchlit blur.

"I think I've got the hang of it now," said Dad, just as *La Poubelle* reversed into the second jousting barge, breaking it almost in two.

"Aaaaaarr! Time to board!" yelled Darius, and before Nat could stop him, he jumped from *La Poubelle* on to the newly bashed-in barge.

The mood of the crowd was changing; Nat could hear cheers turning to jeers. This stupid ugly barge was funny at first, but now it was spoiling things. The lovely boats were being smashed to pieces. This was too much.

The rowers on the boarded boat thought *Darius* was too much too. All but one dropped their oars and dived overboard. One decided to stand and fight.

"Come on, you scurvy dog," said Darius, waving his stick.

"You 'ave ruined everyzink!" shouted the Frenchman, feet swimming in cold water. He grabbed a spare jousting pole from the deck and ran full-tilt at the mini pirate. It caught Darius in the stomach and he went up in the air.

"Pffft," went the tiny buccaneer, making a noise like a leaky tyre. He grabbed on to the pole and dangled there like a ripe fruit. The pole man tried to shake him off, but Darius clung on – and then started clambering down the pole like a starving monkey hunting a banana.

Through the swirling smoke, his enemy saw the boy heading towards him, screamed and tossed the pole as high as he could, out of the boat. Darius plopped into the water.

By now, the marina looked like a rubbish re-enactment of a great naval battle.

"*Not since Ze Battle of Trafalgar has ze French navy fought so bravely and so well,*" declared the man on the Tannoy. The mayor grabbed him angrily.

"We LOST zat battle, you imbecile," he said.

"Well, we are losing zis one too," said the announcer. Their words echoed across the battlefield because they still had the microphone on.

He was right. The French were on the losing side. Both the jousting boats were slowly sinking. The shipwrecked seamen shook their fists at Dad. A few of them swam towards the barge with what Nat reckoned was murder in their hearts.

"I wonder where Rocky is?" asked Dad. "Oh, give Darius a hand to get back on board, will you?"

Nat hauled Darius up. He lay on the deck like a wet rat.

But he wasn't the only one coming on board. A large strong hairy hand came over the rail of the barge. Then another. Nat screamed.

A head came up. It was Rocky! Nat watched as the sodden sailor emerged from the water to lie, gasping, next to Darius. He coughed up a small fish, belched wetly, and said: "That's better."

He's come for revenge! thought Nat, running to the back of the boat, where Dad was still trying to figure out the rudder. "Dad – Rocky is…" she gabbled, trying to tell him Rocky was on board and probably coming to murder him AT LEAST, but Dad wasn't listening.

Dad wasn't listening because he was too busy avoiding ALL THE ROTTEN FRUIT.

The shower of fruit came from the crowd. All the friends of the shipwrecked boaters had gone through the bins to show their support and friendship. And what says friendship more than a rotten tomato?

Dad somehow avoided the worst of the veg. Nat didn't.

SPLAT!

"Not fair," she whined, as one squidgy vegetable after another smashed into her head.

"Ignore it," said Dad, as a tomato caught her full in the face. "It's probably a hilarious French tradition."

"They hate us, Dad."

"Don't be silly. We have as much right to be here as anyone else. If I've learned one thing from Rocky, it's that. We should be more like him."

"I don't want you to be like Rocky, you're even more embarrassing when you try to be like Rocky," said Nat, bits of red tomato dripping from her hair and down her nose, as if to prove her point.

"Head wound, emergency!" shouted Rocky, dashing forward and grabbing her.

"Eeeek," went Nat as she was tipped horizontally. Rocky barked out orders for bandages and compresses and a needle and thread. Dad, suddenly worried, immediately left the rudder to find the first-aid box.

Rocky steered the barge with his foot, still holding the tomato-covered Nat. "Get off me," she said angrily, trying to wriggle free, but her voice was muffled. Rocky had his huge hands round her head, trying to find the nonexistent wound.

"Get off her," said Darius, who jumped on

Rocky's back and grabbed him round the head, trying to prise him off.

"Get off him," said Dad, trying to pull Darius off Rocky.

"Get off ze boat NOW," came a very loud voice through a megaphone. In all the chaos, no one had noticed a blue flashing light. It was the river police, who had pulled up alongside the barge in a little motor boat.

Nat was the first to react. She was so slippywith rotten fruit she slithered out of Rocky's arms, jumped up and shouted: "I don't know who any of these people are."

"Nor me," said Darius.

"Shut up, Darius," she said. "And don't say anything either, Dad, you'll only make it worse."

Then she realised she'd said 'Dad' and 'Darius', and threw herself to the deck in despair.

Around her was utter carnage. One wooden jousting barge was underwater, the other was sinking fast. The crowd were booing, the mayor was being led away in tears and the barge looked like a fruit and veg stall run by a drunk orang-utan.

A soaked Darius and Rocky were grappling on deck, and Nathalia was lying in a miserable, smelly, sodden heap.

"I suppose it's like this every year?" asked Dad, hoping the answer was 'yes'.

"*Non*," said a policeman, taking them all away.

They weren't locked up for very long – the Chief of Police owed Rocky a favour.

"It wasn't getting locked up that bothered me the most, Dad," hissed Nat as they all trooped out of the police station the next morning, "it was getting locked up with YOU."

She noted with satisfaction that at least Rocky didn't seem very friendly towards Dad any more. So it wasn't all bad news.

The walk back to the marina was AWFUL. Nat knew the whole town was staring at her. The front cover of the local paper had HER tomato-covered face on it. She knew because Darius bought six copies.

She was too embarrassed to look properly at the newspaper picture, else she might have seen, there in the crowd, a nasty face of someone she knew. A very suspicious face…

Back at the barge, under the stares of the angry townspeople, Dad agreed with Nat that it was time they were moving on. Rocky said, stiffly, that was probably for the best. Emily smiled and kissed Nat. Then patted Darius on the head, before wiping her hands.

What Nat didn't see was the note that Rocky slipped into her rucksack as they were saying goodbye. He put the envelope into one of her school books that she insisted on bringing with her. He probably thought she opened it regularly. Which proved he wasn't right about *everything*. Nat *never* opened her school books on holiday.

She just liked to carry them around, hoping the information would somehow seep into her.

The note lay undisturbed in her bag for some time.

CHAPTER EIGHTEEN

• • • •

NAT RECKONED MORNINGS WERE THE BEST. BIRDS SANG, ducks quacked, mist rose lazily from the still water. Shafts of pale early light sliced through tall trees. Nat would watch from her cabin as the sun's rays burned off the mist and revealed a sparkling, untouched new day.

Before Dad had a chance to ruin it.

Nat had got used to the fact that they would be a laughing stock wherever they went. And worse, a menace. Dad *still* hadn't got the hang of driving the barge and Nat lost count of the number of times he drove over canoeists, or dragged fishermen into the water by running over their fishing lines. Or just simply fell in himself.

She made a mental note never to look on YouTube for anything with the words:

British. Idiot. Canal. France. Epic Fail.

In the end, she took over most of the steering, although she wasn't really old enough. So between worrying about steering and worrying about *not being seen* steering, she was a nervous wreck by the end of a day.

Darius was another trial. He didn't like confined spaces so every time the boat stopped he would jump off and 'explore'.

Which meant, 'disappear for a couple of worrying hours'. Then, just as they were about to call for search and rescue, he would turn up with a 'souvenir'.

These included: three road signs, a paddling pool, a mobility scooter and a tortoise.

They made him take everything back except one road sign, which pointed the way to a town called:

La Butte ès Gros.

Which they all agreed was too hilarious not to keep.

In one town they passed through, Nat made Dad buy a pay-as-you-go mobile so she could call Mum.

It was hard to get reception though, and Mum was also travelling a lot, so it was IMPOSSIBLE to get hold of her. One night Nat left a message in which she said:

"Mum, we're having what is literally the opposite of a really nice time. Dad thinks he's a brilliant sailor. Darius never behaves himself. Even the Dog is unhappy. I want to come home; it feels like I'm doomed to stay here forever."

But they were in the middle of nowhere and reception was terrible so what Mum heard was:

"Mum, we're having… a really nice time. Dad… 's a brilliant sailor. Darius… behaves himself. The Dog is… happy. I want to… stay here forever."

But all good things come to an end, as do really horrible things, fortunately. And finally, in glorious sunshine, the great day came. Dad parked for the last time. Dad fell in, for the last time.

They were here. Nat half expected everyone on the canal to throw a party to celebrate their leaving.

There waiting for them, as planned, was Dad's pride and joy – the Atomic Dustbin. When the mechanic asked if they'd "'ad any trubble" Dad just said, in his best French:

"I do nurt zink zo. Burt now I 'ave ze big howse to fix and so I sink zat ze trouble is only just starting!"

Despite the warm sun, Nat suddenly felt very cold indeed.

Posh Barry's house was about a mile from the nearest village, down a white, windy-windy road that snaked in between tall, slim trees.

The nearer they got to the house, the smaller the road got and the closer together were the trees. Their branches met, just above the Atomic Dustbin. It was as if they were in a dark green tunnel. The van brushed branches on both sides with a 'shushing' sound.

"Are you sure this is the right way?" asked Nat.

"Satnav says so," said Dad. He was very proud of his second-hand satnav, which he had bought off the internet. It was propped up on the windscreen, and the arrow was green, which meant they were going the right way.

"Blinky blonky hurdy gurdey," said the satnav. In Norwegian.

"I told you to let Darius set it up," said Nat. "Haven't you changed the language yet?"

"Not really. The instructions to change the language are in Norwegian too."

"Manky blanket smurf," said the satnav.

"I think that means turn next left, Dad," said Nat. "That's the way the arrow's pointing."

"See?" said Dad happily, turning down an even smaller road. "You'll come back speaking French

AND Norwegian. I call that a result."

Behind them, a horn blared, making Nat jump. She looked out of the back window and saw a little moped, very close behind, weaving across the road, trying to overtake. But there was no room.

"What shall I throw at him?" asked Darius, as the horn blared again.

"Just throw him a happy smile and a wave," said Dad. "Not THAT kind of wave," said Dad, seeing what Darius was doing with his fingers. The moped's horn blared again.

"You'd think he owned the blinking road," said Dad, pulling over into a driveway to let the annoying moped go by. As it buzzed by them, Nat realised that the rider was *no older than her*. And worse, he was returning Darius's rude wave in the same rude fashion. With extra rudeness on top.

Before they could react, the Norwegian satnav sprang into life: "Flem snotbag curdle fruitbat."

"Looks like we're here!" said Dad. "This is the

drive. Pop out and open the gate, would you?"

Nat looked at an old wooden gate, hanging forlornly off rusty hinges. As she watched, the vibrations from the engine shook the gate clean off.

"It's open," she said flatly.

She hopped back in the van and they drove on. The long drive was overgrown by thick hedges. Branches bashed and scratched at the windscreen.

"It's like they're trying to get in," said Darius. "I saw this film once about trees that liked to munch people."

"I saw that," said Dad. "Scary, wasn't it? They said it was based on a true story."

"Shut up, you two," said Nat. "You're not making this any better."

Just then the trees parted to reveal a large, untidy clearing. And there, finally, they got their first view of the house.

CHAPTER NINETEEN

• • • •

NO ONE SPOKE FOR A FULL MINUTE. DAD TURNED the engine off. Even HE couldn't think of anything to say.

Once she'd recovered from the shock, Nat could.

"What a dump."

"It's not THAT bad," fibbed Dad. "It needs a bit of a tidy-up. I, er, I can definitely probably do this."

They stared at it a while longer. But the more they looked, the worse it got. And the more worried Nat became. This was a BIG JOB.

It was a big house; big and ugly and uncared-for. It was squat and square, with walls of crumbly yellow stone. Straggly green ivy crawled up one side, clawing at the walls.

"It's like the earth is trying to hide it," said Nat.

There were lots of large, rectangular windows, shut up with weathered green shutters, squeaking and creaking on rusty hinges. There was an orange tiled roof, and even from a distance it was obvious that many of the tiles were loose and cracked. In the middle of the roof stood a crooked chimney, leaning like a drunken sailor in a gale. It looked like a gnat's cough could blow it over.

There was a large, peeling red front door, which reminded Nat of a nasty open mouth.

In front of the house lurked a pond, green with old slime. A rusty metal fountain in the shape of a mermaid on a big shell sat dry and forlorn and mouldy in the middle.

"Where's the pool?" said Nat, fearing she already knew the answer.

"Perhaps he only said he *wanted* a pool..." said Dad cheerfully. "Once we finish the house we can dig one."

Nat groaned.

The three of them and the Dog got out of the van and walked slowly up to the house. Gravel crunched under their feet, as did bits of broken glass. It was a hot day and Nat felt a warmth coming from the old stone. The sweet smell of flowers and herbs mingled with the musty pong of the pond.

"I'll tell you what I think," said Darius, eventually.

This will be good, thought Nat. *Darius knows some fantastic swear words.*

"I think this is brilliant."

Nat was about to tell him to shut up, then she remembered the horrible estate where Darius lived.

"Posh Barry said he left the front door key under a pot," said Dad, hunting around.

"Why did he lock it?" said Nat. "No one's gonna want to break into THIS."

"Maybe it was to stop something breaking *out*," said Darius in his best creepy voice. NOW Nat could tell him to shut up.

Nat creaked open a shutter and peeked through

a grimy downstairs window into the living room. It was dark and dusty, but there was a big sofa that looked comfy, and a carved stone fireplace and pretty tiles on the floor. Perhaps it wasn't so bad…

"I've found the pots," said Dad, from round the side of the house. There was a pause. "So now…" he said, "I just have to look under them. Yup, just pick up a pot and look under it. Under, under, under…"

Nat and Darius came up to him, as he stood dithering over a jumbled collection of big stone pots. "What's the matter?" teased Nat, knowing full well what the matter was.

Spiders were what the matter was. Dad HATED spiders. And spiders loved hanging around under pots.

"Nothing," said Dad. "Just wondering which pot the key is under."

"Only one way to find out," said Darius, immediately lifting up a big one.

"Spider, spider, massive spider," said Dad,

jumping back several feet in alarm, "and look at its teeth!"

"It's just a bunch of keys," said Nat, bending down and grabbing them.

"I knew that," said Dad, taking the heavy pot off Darius, who was struggling to hold it.

"HERE'S a spider," said Darius, holding out a big one that had just crawled up his arm.

"Aaaarrgh!" screamed Dad, dropping the big solid, HEAVY pot.

On his foot.

"Aaaarrgh!" screamed Dad again, hopping around on one leg. "Why did I wear sandals today?"

He hopped around the front of the house, trying not to say rude words in front of the children.

"Gah – fnuh – ishhh," he shouted in a strangulated kind of way. Nat giggled; she never minded Dad looking daft as long as no one else saw him.

But...

"Can I help you?" said a polite but unfriendly voice. It was definitely French but its English was near perfect.

"Not unless you can mend toes," said Dad, still hopping about.

"I do hope you haven't broken anything," the voice continued. Nat and Darius came from the side of the house and looked at the speaker. He was a tall man in a dark suit with a thin hooked nose and a high, superior kind of forehead. He looked like an angry hawk.

"Well I can't tell without an X-ray," said Dad, rubbing his sore toes.

"No, not your foot, I don't care about your foot. I mean, I hope you haven't broken anything in my house."

"How could I, I don't even know where your house is," said Dad crossly.

"ZIS is my house," said the man.

At this point Dad realised that the newcomer was French, so started talking to him in Dad French.

"Ah do nurt know what you min," said Dad. "Zis iss mah friend Posh Barry's 'owse. You are barking up ze wrong gumtree, mister."

"Dad, he speaks better English than you," said Nat. "Talk properly."

The Dog sniffed the man, who gave him a dark look and the cowardly mutt slunk off to find somewhere warm to sleep.

The stranger held out a thin bony hand to Dad. "Let me explain," he said. His voice was like silk sliding gently over a razor blade. "My name is Baron du Canard. I own all the land around here. My ancestor, the first Baron, won it after the glorious Battle of Agincourt."

"Hang on," said Nat, who liked history, "the French *lost* that battle. The English won."

"The Baron fought for the English," said the man, with a shrug. "He was a terrible traitor – but a very good businessman."

"Never mind all that," said Dad. "My mate Posh Barry bought this house last year, off an old lady."

"Yes but the old lady was SUPPOSED to sell it to me," the Baron replied angrily. "It's on the only bit of land I don't own around here."

"So you DON'T own the house," said Nat smartly.

The man realised he'd said too much. "No. But I should," he replied.

"But you don't," said Dad. "That settles it."

"Tough banana, Baron Big Nose," said Darius, "so off you trot."

The man looked at him coldly. "The only people trotting off," he said, "will be you. Enjoy your stay. If you want me, I'm in the chateau next door." He turned on his heels and walked quickly off into the woods.

"*If you want me, I'm in the chateau next door*," mimicked Nat. "What a creep."

"Right, never mind the welcome committee," said Dad, "let's go in and see what needs doing." He unlocked the door, yanked it hard and the knob came off. Dad put his hand through the letterbox and pulled.

There was a crash as the door fell on him.

"We should probably start with the door," he said, lying down under it.

CHAPTER TWENTY

• • • •

STEPPING INSIDE THE LONG GLOOMY HALLWAY, NAT could easily see how this house had once been quite grand. The floor was decorated with little patterned tiles, now black with grime. The ceiling was high, with thick wooden beams slathered in dust and cobwebs.

Downstairs there were two large shabby sitting rooms, with peeling, patterned wallpaper and exposed, dangerous-looking wiring.

"Do NOT touch the light switches," said Dad. "In fact, best not touch anything at all." He sounded nervous.

At the back of the house, the large, stone-tiled kitchen had a huge open fireplace. "We could roast a pig in here," said Darius, jumping in the fireplace. "Or torture the Baron."

His voice boomed up the chimney. "Come out of there," said Nat, who wanted a look herself. She stuck her head in and a huge block of soot smacked her full in the face.

"I'll get you for that," she spluttered, wiping the grime from her eyes. Darius dashed out of the kitchen and up a large, curving staircase, Nat following right behind. Each step creaked and groaned as they flew upwards.

The children paused on the long landing upstairs. The doors to the bedrooms were all closed and the only window was tightly shuttered. The whole landing was dark and quiet, like a tomb. Nat shivered. She looked at Darius and wondered why he'd stopped. She had never known him to be afraid of ANYTHING, not even L'Shaun Wiggins, the terror of Year 10, OR the school's shepherd's pie.

There's a first time for everything, she thought. *Maybe, Darius Bagley, you're not so different after all.*

"The ghost is DEFINITELY through *that* door," said Darius, taking a sudden run at it. "Quick, before it disappears."

No, you are very *different*, Nat corrected herself.

Darius hurled himself at the door.

Bang! went Darius. And then *OOF!* went Darius as he bounced off with a crash. It was a very solid door.

"All the bedroom doors are locked tight," shouted Dad, from downstairs. "The place used to be a bed and breakfast, didn't I tell you?"

There were a lot of locked doors. And Nat had a nasty feeling they all hid horrible things. Never mind a ghost, they probably all needed LOADS of DIY doing.

Dad, once again, looked doomed.

Some hours later they had been through the whole house. It seemed bigger on the inside than the outside. There were rooms everywhere; it was like a rabbit warren.

"Or a monster's lair," said Darius with relish.

You would know, thought Nat.

And yes, as Nat had suspected, all the rooms were grotty.

The only room they hadn't been in was a room at the top of the house whose door they couldn't find a key for.

This made Nat very nervous.

"What do you think is in there? Don't you think it's creepy?" she said to Darius later, as they sat in the kitchen drinking pop.

"The whole HOUSE is creepy," said Darius. "Good, innit? Whoever built this place knew what ghosts like."

Nat was surprised that Dad didn't panic about how much work it was going to be. Instead, he carefully made a list of all the DIY jobs that needed doing. Then he put the pencil behind his ear because THAT WAS WHAT BUILDERS DID.

Nat had a horrible suspicion that that was as much as Dad knew about builders. Or DIY.

Nat and Darius were grubby and tired. They were sitting at a large, battered wooden table in the big, ramshackle kitchen. They were at the back of the house and through an outsized window with six huge panes they could see the inviting, overgrown garden.

In the distance, half-hidden in trees, they could just make out a couple of pointy turrets. Nat guessed it was the Baron's chateau.

Darius was whittling a stick into a point with his little knife.

"Another jabbing stick?" asked Nat disapprovingly.

"It's a stake for the Baron's heart," he said cheerfully. "He's obviously a vampire."

"A daytime vampire?"

"Maybe he's wearing lots of sunscreen," said Darius with a shrug. "But I'm not taking any chances."

Nat sighed and looked at Dad who was half under the large stone sink hammering at some green-crusted pipes.

"I'll have the water running again in no time," he shouted. "Get ready to put the kettle on. We can't do anything without a cup of tea."

There was A LOT to do.

In fact, there was so much to do, they had ALL written TO DO lists.

Dad's list:
Fix plumbing.
Fix electrics.
Fix ceilings, windows, stairs, boiler, floorboards, roof, fountain.
Redecorate.
Find out where the smell's coming from.
Buy new net for the ping-pong table.

"A pretty short list, when you write it all down," Dad had said.

Nat's list:

Demolish house.

Buy net for the ping-pong table.

Darius's list was more positive. It read:

Turn house into an evil base for our doomsday
weapon.

Build doomsday weapon.

Buy new net for the ping-pong table.

"How long have we actually got before Posh Barry comes?" said Nat. "Bearing in mind it took you two years to put the lights in my doll's house. And another six months to fix the damage you made putting the lights in."

"Ah well," said Dad, still clanging away at something under the sink. "I've got this theory that things take as long as the time you have to do them."

"You what?" said Nat irritably.

"If you have a weekend to do your history homework, it takes you a weekend, right? If I have six months to write six Christmas cracker jokes, it takes me six months."

Nat knew Dad was avoiding the question. "How long, Dad?" she asked again.

"A whole long week," said Dad, trying to make that sound like ages. "Which means it'll be done in a week. Good job we haven't got six months to do it, right?"

Nat banged her head on the table. "ONE WEEK?" she yelled. "Dad, I've seen you try DIY before, you won't have worked out how to open the toolbox in one week."

"That toolbox was faulty," said Dad defensively.

"Posh Barry and Even Posher Linda will turn up and nothing will be fixed and Mimsy will tell EVERYONE at school that you're a TOTAL FAILURE. And she'll put pictures on her blog and then we're all DOOMED forever."

"Trust me," said Dad, "I know exactly what to do."

"Really?" said Nat hopefully.

"Yes, I'm making us all a nice cuppa. Things will look better after that. I just need to get this water running."

There was a horrible final *clang* and Dad emerged from under the sink, face filthy with old grease and mystery under-the-sink dirt. He tried the taps but they just coughed and shook. A trickle of rusty water eventually plopped out.

"Hmmmm," said Dad. He flicked through a few pages of his old DIY book.

"Is the water turned on from outside?" asked Darius. "There's usually a tap out the back. Oswald once fell out with the whole street and we spent the night turning everyone's water off."

"That's quite funny," said Nat.

"It was so they would burn faster when he set them on fire," Darius explained.

"Yeah, not so funny now," said Nat.

"It was funny when I hid his lighter," said Darius, chuckling. "You should have seen him jumping about."

"Darius, help me find the tap," said Dad. "Nat, read about plumbing. It can't be that difficult."

Dad and Darius went out the back door and Nat flicked through Dad's stupid DIY book. It was full of pictures of useful-looking men with tool belts and check shirts who looked like they knew EXACTLY WHAT THEY WERE DOING. They looked like Rocky.

They were the opposite of Dad.

Nat knew the only DIY book with Dad's picture in would be the 'Don't let this idiot anywhere near a power tool' book.

She put the book down and peered under the sink. There were a lot of bent pipes that didn't look anything like they did in the book. There were bits of screws and bolts and metal rings that looked quite useful that Dad had unscrewed and left in a heap.

Nat wondered if they were important bits.

Then there was a rumbling noise. The floor under her shook. The pipes rattled and coughed and something that sounded like a waterfall rushed towards her.

She heard Dad shout: "I think that's done it – well done, Darius!"

Then a huge jet of water burst out of a pipe under the sink, hitting Nat directly in the stomach.

"WAAAH!" she yelled as the power of the water lifted her clean off her feet and rocketed her straight out of the back door.

"WAAAAAH!" she yelled as she pinged into a pile of old tractor tyres that had been dumped in the garden.

"WAAAAAAAH!" she yelled, as she bounced off the tyres and straight up in the air. She did a half-somersault and fell head-first, back into the tyres. All that could be seen of her were two little feet sticking up, wriggling furiously.

"That looks cool," said Darius, grabbing her legs. "My turn next."

He yanked on her feet and she slithered out, soaking wet and covered in tyre muck and garden slime. She lay panting on the grass for a moment. She heard a high-pitched noise and shook the water out of her ears. The water came out but the annoying noise was still there.

She looked around and eventually saw a boy, about her age, up a nearby tree.

HA HA HA HA HA HA HA HAA

"Ha ha ha ha, zat is very funny, ha ha ha, stupid English idiot," said the boy.

He was laughing and pointing at her. She couldn't be sure at this distance but he looked a lot like the annoying boy on the moped.

She shouted something rude back at him. Darius didn't seem to care. He was scrabbling about in a pile of old rubbish and bits of broken crockery nearby.

He seemed very interested in an old dinner plate.

"Thanks for sticking up for me," said Nat. But Darius just smiled, and then with a powerful throw, launched the plate like a discus.

It whizzed through the air, spinning so fast it made a humming noise. It was a brilliant shot, heading straight for the boy, who saw it hurtling towards him and gave a shrill shriek. The boy dodged out of the way, but slipped off the branch and disappeared into a bush. A cloud of ducks flew up, quacking in alarm.

For a few seconds there was silence. Nat turned to Darius, who had lost interest in the proceedings and was wandering off. "Do you think he's still alive?"

Just then they heard him cry: "*PAPA, Papaaaa!*"

Guess so, she thought. And then, *Oh dear, I wonder who his papa is…*

CHAPTER TWENTY-ONE

••••

OW THAT THE WATER WAS BACK ON, IT WAS EASY TO see where the leaks were.

The leaks were everywhere.

The kitchen pipes leaked, the bathroom pipes leaked, the boiler leaked. After running around with buckets for an hour or so, Nat shouted: "I've counted *sixty-four* leaks."

"Sixty-four," shouted Darius, running about. "Brilliant number." Nat looked at him. They'd driven to a café earlier and filled a flask of strong coffee for Dad. Nat had a sneaking suspicion Dad would find it empty. Darius was bouncing off the walls, literally.

Very rarely, Darius would let it slip that he LOVED numbers.

"It's the square of eight, it's the cube root of… two hundred and sixty-two thousand, one hundred and forty-four." He skidded to his knees in the hallway like a footballer who's just scored. "Go, Dariusssssssss."

"Why don't you ever show you can do maths at school?" asked Nat. She had only found out that Darius was a maths genius by accident, and now always got him to do her maths homework for her.

But Darius immediately stopped playing with numbers as soon as she brought attention to it. "It's none of their business," he said.

Nat sighed and gave up.

"I don't remember drinking all that coffee," said Dad, peering into his flask.

Dad had decided to take a break. The three of them sat on the stairs, listening to lots of drips in lots of buckets.

The water was running now. Running and dripping. In fact the only place in the house where there *wasn't* water was the loo.

"And that's the one place where there definitely *should* be water, Dad," complained Nat unnecessarily. "What are you going to do about the leaks?"

"Technically, you could say the leaks are fixed," said Dad. "As long as you keep the buckets under them."

"Posh Barry is not going to think you've fixed the leaks just by putting buckets out," said Nat.

"You might have a point, love," said Dad. "What does the DIY book say?"

"Dad, you've had AGES to swot up on this," Nat said. "Haven't you learned anything?"

"I don't NEED to learn it," Dad said. "It's in the book."

"That's what I said about my history homework and you still made me learn it."

Dad didn't reply, he just flicked through the

'plumbing problems' section.

"Here we are," he said. He read for a while. Nat watched his face and wondered how long it would take for him to look bored. She counted thirty seconds and then saw Dad's eyes glaze over.

"Concentrate, Dad," she said. Dad tried again.

He nearly lasted a whole minute.

"Dad, you said you could do this."

She kicked at a loose tile on the floor in frustration. The best thing about holidays was that Dad only embarrassed her in front of people she'd never see again. But as soon as that awful spoilt Mimsy arrived and posted a photo of the house on her blog (MimsysModestBlog.com), all her friends would read it and her dad would be revealed as a complete idiot to the WORLD. Nat had only just started making friends at her school. This could set her back YEARS.

BUT THEN:

Dad suddenly jumped up, scaring the Dog who'd been dozing under his feet.

"I DID say I can do it, and I CAN!" he

declared heroically. "I'm going to tackle each leak in turn until it's done. What we need is some determination, some action, and some good old-fashioned hard work, RIGHT NOW."

"Brilliant, Dad!" said Nat, eager to start.

"We'll just pop into the village for some supper and we'll start tomorrow," he said.

"No, Dad, start NOW!" she yelled. "We haven't got TIME to mess about."

Dad looked at Nat's determined, cross little face. He smiled. "All right, love. How hard can it be?" he said. He marched out like a lion, clutching his toolbox.

By nightfall he was lying on the sofa, soaking wet and filthy. There were even MORE buckets around, catching more drips.

"Well," he said miserably, "it appears that plumbing is REALLY hard. I think I might have made it a tiny bit worse. I got confused between inches and centimetres when I was putting some pipe in and now there's more water on the bathroom floor than IN the bath I've been trying to run."

Nat felt like weeping.

"Maybe you should start with the electrics," said Darius, "and work up to the plumbing."

"Sensible lad," said Dad, dozing off.

When Dad woke up from his nap, they had a gloomy supper of dry, leftover sandwiches Dad had bought in the café earlier that day, and then they all went to bed.

Nat had bagsied the least scary-looking room, with pretty, faded rose-print wallpaper, a little fireplace and a big brass bed. She opened the shutters and decided that the moonlight made the room look almost cheerful.

Maybe this house just needs a bit of love, she thought, crawling into her sleeping bag on the mattress.

She could hear Dad snoring in one room and the still wide-awake Darius chanting, "Here, ghosty ghost…" in another.

What the house does NOT need is those two,

she thought, dropping off almost immediately, only to be awoken five minutes later by water dripping on her nose. She was so tired and fed up, she just rolled out of bed and went to sleep with the Dog.

"This is NOT my idea of a good holiday," muttered Nat the next morning, for the eighty-sixth time since they'd left home. They were in the kitchen finishing off the now completely stale leftover sandwiches from yesterday. Nat watched as Darius built a frightening-looking sculpture out of wood and wire. She knew he wasn't going to ask *her* what her idea of a good holiday was, so she told him.

"A beach, a pool, sunbeds, my music and Wi-Fi," she listed. "Instead I've got plumbing and hammering and wiring and painting."

And panic and worry and misery, she added, in her head.

"And ghost-catching," said Darius. "THAT's a good holiday." His contraption slammed shut with a wicked clang.

Ah, so that's what it is, thought Nat.

"Do something useful, and shut up about ghosts," she said. "You'll summon them up and it'll be your fault if I get ghost-munched."

Just then there was a tremendous hammering on the front door. The doorknob rattled. Nat jumped, then realised it was real, live people outside.

I wouldn't pull on the front door, she thought, *it might fall on you*.

The door fell on them.

Told you, she thought, popping out of the kitchen to investigate. Dad was helping the Baron du Canard out from under the door. With him Nat could see was the young boy who had been up the tree yesterday.

Obviously the flipping Baron's his dad, she thought... She quickly scooted out of sight, but not so far that she couldn't hear.

First, there was the usual shouting at Dad that she knew so well. *It starts with shouting*, she thought. *By the end of the week it'll be villagers with flaming torches.*

Darius came and sat next to her, messing with his trap. He listened for a while.

"Another word for my rude foreign word collection," he said, pleased. "I'm going to make it into a book and make zillions. If you help me with the spelling, I'll split the cash with you. As long as I get to do the drawings."

"Drawings?" said Nat.

"Yeah, to show how rude the words really are. I've already started some on the landing walls. Look…" he said, showing her some REVOLTING biro scribbles.

Nat knew she should be cross, but she started to giggle. They were VERY rude. "We'll just tell Dad that burglars did them," she said.

"Or ghosts," said Darius, a gleam in his eye. "Ghosts can't resist drawing on walls. I saw a film about it."

Downstairs, Dad took the angry visitors into the kitchen and they could no longer hear what was going on.

"He'll wiggle out of it. I don't know how he does it, but he does."

Ten minutes later, she found out how. She was called into the kitchen.

"This is the Baron's son, little Gaston," said Dad, indicating a squat freckled child with thin lips and thick black curls. "We decided that to prove there're no hard feelings, he's going to be your new best friend."

The three children looked at each other without saying anything. It was less like a meeting of new best friends and more like a shoot-out at the end of a cowboy movie.

After the Baron and Gaston had left, Dad explained excitedly:

"This is a brilliant plan. No one in the village likes Gaston because he's so horrible."

"Why's that brilliant?" said Nat.

"Because he has no friends and the Baron doesn't know what to do with him. So all you have to do is play with him and keep him entertained and the Baron will help us."

"Help us how?" said Nat suspiciously.

"He's got loads of workmen at his chateau, and he's said he might lend us some. For FREE."

"No, Dad, not for free," argued Nat. "WE'RE paying, aren't we?"

"PLAYING, not PAYING!" said Dad, gently pushing them outside into the late afternoon sunshine. "Now, just remember, Gaston has to win every game, all the time, OK? How hard can that be?"

CHAPTER TWENTY-TWO

• • • •

IT WAS VERY, VERY HARD.

All day they played every game Gaston wanted to. And let him win.

For Nat, the only thing harder than letting him win was making sure *Darius* let him win. Darius was different from most people. Most people don't like being told what to do; Darius didn't understand what being told what to do WAS.

So:

When they played races, Nat had to pretend to fall over, and then 'accidentally' trip Darius up.

When they played throwing, Nat had to drop the ball and nudge Darius's arm.

When they played football, Nat had to score five own goals and send Darius off.

And when they played hide-and-seek, Nat had to hide really badly and tell Gaston where Darius was.

Basically, Nat made herself look *a complete idiot.*

Thanks again, Dad, she thought.

And all the time, the French boy bragged and boasted. He went to a posh school in a castle, he had his own moped, he was a champion skier, a brilliant tennis player and an *amazing* horse rider. On and on he went.

But then, on their tenth game of hide-and-seek, when Nat told Gaston that Darius was hiding in the old chicken coop under a stinky pile of straw and feathers, Gaston just said:

"Let's leave him there, and we'll play without him."

Nat didn't know what to do. She didn't want

to upset THIS little monster, but she didn't want to abandon HER little monster either.

Life's tricky, she thought. A piercing whistle, like a huge duck surprised by a shark, split the air. Gaston jumped, as if he was frightened.

"It's Papa," he said. "He loves his ducks. He breeds the best ducks in France. That's how he calls them." He lowered his eyes. When he lifted them Nat saw for the first time they were a tiny bit sad. "It's how he calls *me* too," he said.

And ran off.

Whoa. At least my dad doesn't do that, I suppose, thought Nat.

And then a huge sticky mess hit the back of her head, and stinky chicken feathers sprayed around her. "That's for spoiling every game, BUTTFACE," said Darius, who had just lobbed a handful of the most vile mixture imaginable at her that he'd scraped up from the floor of the chicken coop.

"You are SO dead, Bagley," yelled Nat, chasing him. She felt much better about everything after she'd ground his face into some grass.

"Dunno about you two, but I could do with a bath," said Dad that evening as the pair finally trudged in.

Dunno about us two? thought Nat. *Have you SEEN us two?*

They looked like a cross between a vegetable patch and a chicken with feather mange. They were plastered head to foot with bits of literally *everything* growing. If they had shown up at the Royal Botanic Gardens at Kew looking like that, thought Nat, gardeners would have found new species of plant life in their *ears*.

It took hours to have a bath. 'Having a bath' meant sitting in a big tin tub in about five centimetres of lukewarm water. The only hot water was from a kettle, and that wasn't working too well either.

"I'll have a go at the electrics again tomorrow," promised Dad as they all trooped off to bed, still a bit grubby. "The good news is – wait for it…"

Dad looked very pleased with himself.

"...the Baron is sending a plumber round tomorrow. For free! My cunning plan is working! Go Dad!"

"Well, it's a start, I suppose," said Nat, painfully aware that Posh Barry's arrival was less than a week away.

"Yup, and I've agreed you'll keep playing with Gaston tomorrow; right I'm off to bed, night night," gabbled Dad, practically running up the stairs.

"WHAT?" yelled Nat.

"Get lost, not doing it," shouted Darius.

"No, not you, just Nat, good night!" shouted Dad, hopping into his bedroom and slamming the door shut after him.

"WHAT???" shouted Nat, louder.

"Ha ha. Watch out for my ghost traps!" said Darius, as Nat ran towards Dad's room, furious.

"What ARE you on about?" said Nat. *SNAP!* went a ghost-trap on her foot. "AAAARGH!" she shouted in pain, foot tangled in wires.

This day gets better and better, she thought.

Nat was so tired from all the working, playing and bashing Darius that once she'd got Darius's stupid ghost-trap off her foot and stumbled furiously into her bedroom, she was asleep almost before her head hit the pillow…

…Only to wake up in the middle of the night, lying in a strange bed in a strange house with all the lights flickering on and off in A REALLY SPOOKY WAY.

"Don't worry about the lights!" shouted Dad from the next room. "It's probably just the electrics playing up."

"*Probably*, Dad?" she shouted back. "What do you mean, *probably*?"

"Just go back to sleep," said Dad. "You've got a busy day at the chateau tomorrow."

She thought she heard him chuckle. Nat fumed silently.

"Anyway, you'd be bored here. Darius has to help me with the electrics – he's good with engines. You'll have more fun than us two hard working boys will."

Nat DEFINITELY heard Darius chuckle.

"DAD," said Nat crossly. "One – I don't want to go to the stupid chateau, and two – engines *aren't* electrics."

"One – yes but we need to keep on the Baron's good side, and two – electrics and engines are next to each other in my DIY book."

"One – I know but it's not FAIR, and two – that's only because the book *is in alphabetical order*."

Dad was quiet for a minute after that.

"Well, one AND two – go to sleep, it's late," said Dad. "And don't worry – everything will be fine!"

But now Nat *was* worrying, more than ever. Not only did she have to spend the day with *horrible*, spoilt Gaston, but Dad and Darius were going to be spending the day playing with six bazillion volts of super-dangerous electricity. The ghost was now relegated to THIRD on her ever-growing LIST OF THINGS TO WORRY ABOUT.

But it wasn't third for long.

Nat lay still, trying to sleep. But sleep would not come. She opened her eyes and looked around the room. It had huge windows opening on to the back garden. Thick heavy drapes hung limply across them, making the room stuffy. The flickering lights cast patterns in shadow around the room.

Opposite the bed there was a small dressing table with a cracked jug and dish on. There was a large fireplace which was half uncovered. It was hard to tell if someone was halfway through boarding it up, or halfway through *getting out of it*.

The old pink flowery wallpaper that had seemed so charming in daylight, now looked like the kind of flowers you can boil to make poison. There was a yellowing black and white photograph in a frame on the wall. It was of an old man and woman, wearing thick dark clothing, looking thoroughly disagreeable. Their cold eyes bored into Nat.

Lighten up, guys, she thought, *or I'm turning you over to face the wall.*

Still sleep would not come. She tossed and turned in her sleeping bag and got herself in such a knot that her arms were pinned under herself.

And then, in the darkest of the night, she heard something. A noise from the fireplace. Nat knew it was definitely the wind. Or possibly a horrid blood-sucking ghost.

Oooooh, moaned the noise. All the hair on the back of Nat's neck stood up and tried to run off. Definitely ghost, she decided.

Then came the scrabbling. Either a mouse or a restless evil spirit in the fireplace was TRYING TO ESCAPE!

"GHOST!" she shouted, making a swift choice and struggling to get out of her sleeping bag. In her panic, she got the zip stuck. She was trapped! She rolled off the bed like a big fat quilted worm and wriggled to the door.

"GHOST!" she yelled again. She was SURE that something was in the room behind her. The lights were flickering like mad. She heaved herself upright and tried to turn the doorknob with her teeth. Now something was howling. *Howling?*

"GHOST*AND*WEREWOLF!" she shouted.

"Will you shut that Dog up?" shouted a sleepy Dad.

"OK, just ghost," she corrected herself, "but still, GHOST!"

The door was stuck fast. She was going to have to bash it down. She took a few hops backwards to build up speed and then launched herself straight at it. Just as Darius opened the door.

For the second time since arriving at the house, she went through an open door at speed. This time, though, she took Darius with her. She smacked into him headlong, sending them both sprawling, and straight down the stairs.

"What's all the racket?" shouted Dad, coming out of his room, wearing just a dressing gown.

"AAAAARGH!" yelled Nat, from the bottom of the stairs.

"AAAAARGH!" yelled Darius.

"What is it?" said Dad, alarmed.

"Your dressing gown has come open!" shouted Nat in horror.

"Sorry," said Dad, wrapping his gown tighter. "I thought you must have seen something horrible."

"We have NOW," said Nat. She and Darius picked themselves off the floor, and climbed painfully back up the stairs.

Nat told them both what she'd heard.

"No, that's my room," said Darius as Nat went to his door.

"It's mine now," said Nat. "You wanted to catch the ghost – now's your

chance. It's in MY ROOM; bye. Happy hunting."
And with that, she slammed the door on him.

Darius stood on the landing for a minute.

"Do I at least get the Dog?" he asked.

"No," said Nat through the door firmly.

"Oh, all right," he said. "But I warn you, it's just as spooky in my room."

Nat looked around at the gloomy room she was now in. There was worse wallpaper, creepier pictures and a bigger fireplace. She came out.

"Yeah, that is QUITE spooky," she admitted.

They stood on the landing for a minute, deciding what to do. Then Dad came out of his room too, looking a bit pale. "I don't ACTUALLY believe in ghosts," he said, "but I've been wrong about things before so I'm going to sleep downstairs."

"Good idea," said Nat, racing him to the sofa.

"Good idea," said Darius, racing *her* to the sofa.

"Woof," said the cowardly Dog, beating them all to the sofa.

CHAPTER TWENTY-THREE

· · · ·

THE NEXT MORNING, THE STUCK-UP BARON AND BRATTY little Gaston came to call for Nathalia.

On the doorstep, a tired and achy Nat stood bored while Dad and the Baron did the grown-up, pointless chit-chat that grown-ups who don't really like each other do.

The Baron was showing off, talking snootily about the history of his family name, du Canard.

Oh no, thought Nat.

"It's funny you mentioned names, actually, because ours is also a French name," said Dad.

OH NO, don't tell him, don't tell him...
thought Nat.

The only other good thing about being on holiday with Dad was that NOBODY KNEW HER EMBARRASSING NAME.

"It's Bew—"

"It's Smith," Nat said loudly.

"Don't be silly," said Dad. "Anyone would think you're ashamed of your own name."

Not my name, just YOU, she thought. *For giving me the stupid name.*

"It's *bew-mow-lay*," said Dad, pronouncing it carefully.

OK, I might get away with that, thought Nat. *As long as Dad's not daft enough to spell it.*

"But funnily enough, it's spelled B- U- M- O- L- É," said Dad.

"Ha ha, bum 'ole bum 'ole!" shouted Gaston with glee. "See, Papa, it is one of zose rude English words I learned at school."

"That's money well spent on your education," said the Baron coldly.

"A bum 'ole is a—" began the boy.

"I know what it is," said the Baron, "and, yes, it is *très drôle*. I mean, very 'ilarious."

"Bum 'ole, bum 'ole," chanted Gaston, running around in evil joy.

"Nice one, Dad," said Nat sulkily.

"So, Mister Buttock…" began the Baron.

"*Bew-mow-lay*," corrected Dad.

"Quite so. Apologies," said the Baron, with just a hint of a smirk on his face. "Well, we must be off. When we get back I will send over the plumber to 'elp with your 'ouse. Come along, children."

Just as they were about to leave, Dad took Nat to one side and said encouragingly, "You'll be fine, love. You hang out with Darius all the time, and the Head told me he's the naughtiest boy in the history of your school."

Nat sighed. She knew there was NO WAY Dad could mend this rubbish house without help.

"OK," she said, "but if he calls me names again, I'll punch him in the eye, I don't care how many free workmen we're getting."

She was just about to leave when she remembered something. Dad was doing the electrics that day.

"Promise me you'll wear rubber welly boots. They save you from electric shocks."

"What about me?" said Darius, wandering past, holding a spanner.

"You're indestructible. I've pummelled you all year and you're fine."

"True," said Darius. "Have fun with your new best friend, Buttface."

The chateau lay at the end of a long and well-kept drive. The bright green lawns either side were mowed flat like the top of a snooker table and the house itself was as white as a wedding cake. Nat counted at least thirty windows. There were two little towers at either side of the building, topped by pointy roofs like little witch's hats. At the front of the house were two posh cars, a pickup truck and Gaston's little moped.

The air was filled with quacking from what must have been hundreds of ducks somewhere at the back of the house.

"Hurry up," said Gaston, ushering her into a huge hall that was covered in oak panelling. "We're playing Gaston-opoly. It's a board game I invented myself. I'm brilliant at it and I always win. You're the tortoise and I'm the racing car."

WHAT a surprise, she thought glumly.

The game was spread out on the floor of a huge room downstairs. It looked like the messiest toy shop in the world. The game should have been fun, because Gaston had obviously spent ages making up the rules.

If you rolled a double three times in a row, you had to go into the wardrobe and wear a silly hat. If you landed on a train station, you got to fire up a real miniature steam train and try to get it through a level crossing without it being hit by an escaped elephant from the toy circus.

There was a rule about using a remote-controlled helicopter, a rule about doing a jigsaw, and lots of rules where you got to eat a sweet.

It was a game that could only have been invented by a boy who spent a lot of time alone, thought Nat. And she reckoned it could have been the greatest game in the world. The trouble was, only Gaston got to do the cool stuff. After an hour of politely watching him play with all his toys and eat all the sweets and jump off chairs and run around having an altogether marvellous time, Nat said mildly, "Can I have a go at something fun?"

"NO," screamed the boy, high on sugar and showing off. "You can have fun by watching how awesome I am. You're just a stupid girl, you can't do anything."

That was IT. Nat stood up, tiny fists clenched in trademark fury. All thoughts of free workmen vanished.

"You are NOT awesome," she said, "and I don't know what the French word is, but what you are is a *brat*. And you're about to be a battered brat."

The boy backed into a corner. He wasn't used

to being answered back and he certainly wasn't used to being battered.

Nat pushed him up against the wall. "You've got everything in the world and it's just made you horrible and selfish and mean. It's why you've got no friends, and no one wants to tell you the truth because your dad is big and powerful, but I will *so there*."

The boy shook her off and ran from the room crying, "Papa, PAPA!"

Papa, as it turned out, had been standing in the doorway for... how long?

Ooops, thought Nat.

"Is that the time?" she said innocently. "Didn't know it was so late. I'll just be going..."

"Wait there," said the Baron sternly. "Gaston, go into the kitchen, tell cook to hurry with lunch. And please stop snivelling."

The boy snivelled off. The Baron closed the door. There was a nasty pause. "Well said," he muttered finally.

"You what?" said Nat.

"I don't understand children," said the Baron. "His mother was so much better with him. His mother…"

The Baron hesitated and Nat saw a look of sadness cross his stern face. Then the cloud passed and he was back to normal.

"…And so now I prefer ducks. Much easier to understand," the Baron continued in his usual stiff manner.

Whatevs, thought Nat, who was beginning to have a teeny bit of sympathy for Gaston.

"He's just a kid," she said, "and just because no one likes him doesn't mean he's THAT bad. I mean, no one likes Darius but… OK, that's a bad example…"

The Baron thought for a moment. "I've decided you must stay all day. Maybe you can do him some good. Lunch will be served shortly. I must get back to my ducks. If you are lucky, I may let you see them later."

And with that he strode stiffly out.

Let's hope I'm lucky, thought Nat sarcastically.

I mean, I've been SO lucky already today.

In the hall, the Baron took his duck whistle from his pocket and gave it an enormous honk. Gaston came running up obediently.

"The girl is staying," said the Baron. "Do not embarrass me again."

Gaston looked at the floor. "Don't embarrass *him*?" he muttered, just loud enough for Nat to hear. Nat felt another twinge of sympathy. If *anyone* knew about embarrassing dads, it was her.

CHAPTER TWENTY-FOUR

••••

LUNCH IN THE CHATEAU CAME OUT OF A BIG STEAMING pot. It was delicious, but spoilt by being eaten in grim silence under the stern gaze of the Baron at one end of the long, polished dining table and a red-eyed boy eating furiously at the other. Nat was in the middle, trying to think of something to lighten the miserable mood.

She wished Darius was there. His rude rhymes were hilarious and his ability to make fart noises using any part of his body, including his ears, was hysterical. He could shove a whole bowl of peas up his nose, do farmyard impressions AND sit upside down on his chair at the same time. And that was just normal mealtimes. When he actually TRIED to make people laugh, he was better than any comic off the telly, by miles.

She must have been smiling because the Baron looked at her and said:

"Something amusing you?" He poured himself some wine from a jug shaped like a duck.

"I'm just enjoying myself," she porky-pied quickly.

The Baron frowned. "No one has enjoyed themselves here for a long time. I didn't think I was very good at entertaining children."

"Oh, come on," said Nat, determined to be cheerful, "you've got this huge cool house with tons of stuff in it. And pots of money. You must have fun!"

There was a *very* long pause. The only fun Nat was having was working out how to get revenge on Dad for dropping her in it like this.

"Fun?" said the Baron. "*Fun?*" He rolled the

word round in his mouth, like someone who was tasting something they'd never eaten before.

"Papa has his ducks," muttered Gaston, head down low over his plate. For the first time, Nat noticed all the pictures hung on the kitchen wall were of ducks.

"Yes, but my ducks are not *fun*," corrected the Baron. "Breeding the best ducks in France is my reason for life."

Get a grip, thought Nat, *they're only rubbish ducks*.

"Oh, that's interesting," she said out loud. *Oooh, I'm fibbing loads today*, she thought. "Do they do anything? I mean, are they special ducks? Can they ride bicycles or work out the angles of a triangle?"

There was a strange noise from the boy. It was almost a giggle, but it was over very quickly. Nat could see she was getting herself into proper hot water, but couldn't find a way out.

"Or – are they just, like, ordinary ducks that lay eggs and go quack?"

"This flock is not ordinary! It was started by my great-great-great-great grandfather…" began the Baron, before launching into a very long and very boring story. Basically, Nat quickly worked out they were indeed just ordinary ducks, but they tasted better than other ducks.

"As a matter of interest," she said, a horrible suspicion creeping over her as the Baron finished explaining how he'd given them all names, "what did we just have for lunch?"

"Eric," said the Baron, sucking meat off a bone with a big greasy smack.

There was a huge, delicious-smelling lemon tart for pudding, but Nat had lost her appetite.

After lunch, the Baron disappeared (*probably to slap more sunscreen on*, thought Nat, remembering what Darius had said about him being a vampire) and Gaston took Nat on a tour of the huge house. It was filled with the sort of lovely old things you only ever see on antiques programmes; luxurious leather chairs, crystal vases, silver dishes, burnished wood cabinets with the high gloss of centuries of polish.

Nat noticed Gaston didn't touch ANYTHING. It was as if he was scared to even leave a fingerprint.

She thought about *her* house – all messy and way tinier than this one, full of dog hair and chewed sofas and big squishy chairs and carpets with irremovable tea stains and wallpaper with her old childhood felt-tip pen marks on (soppy Dad was too soft, or too lazy, to remove them). But at least it felt like a *home*.

Now they were in yet another large room, and this one was filled from floor to ceiling with books. There was even a stepladder on wheels to reach the top ones. There must have been thousands, most of them huge and leather-bound, and all lined up neatly on shelves like soldiers on parade. Some looked really old. Nat let out a low whistle.

"Has your dad read ALL of these?" she asked, impressed.

"Of course not," said Gaston, "these aren't for

reading. Papa buys them by the metre, because they look awesome."

Nat thought that was the most ridiculous thing she'd ever heard. She only had one bookcase in her bedroom, but she'd read every book in it, usually two or three times.

"Once Papa wanted to fill a big gap in the shelves so he just bought the whole village library," boasted Gaston.

"Don't you ever go to the village?" Nat asked. "There must be loads of kids to play with there."

"They've stopped playing with me because I win at everything every time because I'm cleverer and faster and better and they get jealous," said Gaston.

Nat decided to tell him the truth once more. She was going to break it to him gently.

"Listen, big head," she said, not very gently at all, "they've stopped playing with you because you're horrible."

Gaston looked shocked. Nat pressed on.

"Everyone *lets* you win because the Baron is

rich and important. But you're not going to make any REAL friends like that."

Gaston wasn't grateful for the advice. He flew into a rage. "I AM brilliant at everything. I beat you AND that horrible boy at races."

"We let you win."

"I beat you at throwing."

"Let you win."

"I beat you at football."

"SO let you win."

"I beat you at hiding."

"Stop it now. NO ONE beats Darius Bagley at hiding."

"I found him."

"Only because I told you where he was."

"Did not, he's a rubbish hider."

Nat was fed up with this. She'd been feeling sorry for Gaston before, but he was clearly a lost cause. "Darius Bagley is SO GOOD at hiding he even hid from Suspicious Mick. And he was a *proper, official* person-finder. That was his job."

"That's not a job," said Gaston.

"Yes, it is," said Nat. "That's how much you know. Suspicious Mick was on the ferry, looking for all the people without passports. And Darius was hiding because he hasn't got one, so there."

"Is that right?" said Gaston, suddenly looking very interested.

"Yeah, so don't tell me Darius isn't great at hiding. And I'm going home now, thank you."

That's told him, thought Nat, as she stomped out of the library. She was glad she'd stood up for Darius. *I wonder if he knows what a good friend I am?* she thought.

Then, as she stormed out, Nat did something very naughty. She noticed the Baron's wretched duck whistle on a carved wooden table in the hall. She snatched it up. *I'll make you jump, you little beast*, she thought, pocketing the object. She'd seen how it scared Gaston and she was going to give him a huge blast when he wasn't expecting it.

It's not stealing, it's only borrowing, she told herself, looking over her shoulder to make sure Gaston hadn't noticed, as she trudged back to

Posh Barry's rubbish leaky haunted house.

Gaston hadn't noticed. He was too deep in thought.

CHAPTER TWENTY-FIVE

• • • •

$\mathbb{B}$ACK AT THE HOUSE, NAT COULDN'T SEE DAD OR Darius anywhere. There was, however, a big cheerful French plumber leaving the kitchen. "Ze 'ot water, she is on," he said, on his way out. "See you tomorrow."

Get in, thought Nat. *I'm off for a bath.*

Nat heard some muffled banging and swearing coming from somewhere, but she couldn't be bothered to look in case she got roped into helping.

I've helped you enough today, Dad, she thought. But just as Nat was running herself a bath, she caught sight of Darius out of the bathroom window, standing in the broken fountain, knee deep in scummy water, doing something with *an electrical cable*. Nat froze. It was insanely dangerous!

"Bagley, you moron!" she shouted. "Remember that YouTube video that I wasn't supposed to watch that you showed me where that man drops an electric toaster in the bath?"

"Oh yeah," laughed Darius, "that was funny."

"Remember what happened to him?"

"The water lit up bright blue, there was a massive bang and he got turned into toast," said Darius.

"SO GET OUT!" shouted Nat.

Dad came running up from somewhere, panting. "Out!" he shouted. Darius hopped on to dry land. "Good lad," said Dad. "I mean, obviously it's SAFE," he said hastily, catching Nat's angry eye as she came storming outside, "but we should probably test it from a distance first."

You two deserve each other, thought Nat. "Dad, what are you actually doing?" she asked. "You said you were fixing the lights today."

"Oh that," said Dad lightly. "It's on my to-do list. But more importantly, I found the plans on how to get the fountain working again."

"That's literally way less important than the lights," said Nat crossly.

"Ah, now that's where you're wrong," said Dad confidently. "First impressions are everything, see? I've watched loads of daytime telly home makeover shows, and they always say that. So when Posh Barry and Even Posher Linda arrive next week, what will be their first impression?"

"That they left their house in the care of an idiot?"

"Apart from that... They'll see their lovely fountain, all working and splashy. They'll be so impressed they might forgive the odd imperfection *inside*."

Nat sighed and gave up arguing. "What's that you've got?" said Darius, pointing to the duck whistle. Nat told him about her day with ghastly Gaston while Dad carried on tinkering with the fountain.

"I think we're about ready to test it," said Dad. "Brace yourselves, I'm putting the power back on."

He disappeared off back into the house.

Brace yourselves? thought Nat. *That doesn't sound good.*

They both stepped back from the fountain.

"Can I have a go?" said Darius, grabbing the whistle out of her hands.

"No," said Nat. "I should put it back really, before I get into trouble. I only took it because I was annoyed. Give it here."

She tried to grab it back.

"Just one blow," said Darius, dodging.

"I said no; I want a go first anyway."

Darius put it to his lips and blew. A feeble farty noise came out. At the same time they heard a sizzling sound.

"That's a funny noise," said Darius, looking at

the whistle.

"No, you moron," she said, "it's the fountain. I think it's actually working."

As they watched, water began to pour out of the bronze mermaid's mouth. Then, slowly at first, thin jets of water began squirting upwards, dancing around her.

"Dad's done it!" said Nat. "I don't believe it."

Dad came running out. He punched the air in triumph. "Go, Dad!" he shouted. "They came to mock – they stayed to applaud."

He walked over to Nat, looking VERY pleased with himself. "And I think you were beginning to doubt your old dad," he said.

"I admit it," Nat said. "The fountain looks great."

It really did. The water was pouring out noisily and columns of water danced upwards. The late afternoon sunlight glinted invitingly off the jets, which looked VERY blue. And was that a sizzling sound again?

"I didn't know there were lights in it, Dad,"

she said, noticing the blue glow.

"There aren't," said Dad, not really paying attention. He was looking at the duck whistle Darius was brandishing. "Can I have a go with that?"

He grabbed it and gave it a series of huge loud honks. Nothing happened for a few seconds and then a cloud of the Baron's prize fat ducks came swooping and flapping into the garden.

Dad laughed and laughed, until the fountain stopped working. The water dribbled to a halt and the blue light went out.

"Loose connection," said Dad, as the ducks landed around them. He went back into the house, and Nat and Darius watched as the fat birds waddled into the fountain, splashing happily as if they'd found a nice new duck pond.

There was some worry lurking at the back of Nat's mind as she watched the happy ducks. Something was terribly wrong, she just couldn't put her finger on it.

Whatever it was, it was quickly forgotten when

she heard the Baron's silky voice behind her.

"There you are, little girl," he said. "I have lost something and I was wondering if you had seen it, by any chance?"

"Haven't seen your whistle," Nat said quickly. Too quickly.

"I didn't say what it was I had lost," he said, smiling thinly.

Eeek, thought Nat.

"Power's coming back on," shouted Dad from inside the house. "Tell me if anything happens."

"And what are you doing with all my ducks?" said the Baron, suddenly noticing them all in the fountain.

"Three…" shouted Dad, counting down.

"Is that why you took my whistle? Are you duck thieves?" said the Baron.

"Two…"

"You know that video of the man in the bath with the toaster?" said Darius, who had just worked out what was about to happen.

"One…"

"NOOOO!" shouted Nat, having just figured it out too.

"ZERO!" shouted Dad, throwing the switch.

ZZZAP! went the electricity, sending ten thousand volts through the metal fountain and instantly frying the ducks.

QUAAAACK! went the shocked ducks, covered in bright blue sparks.

BANG! went the electrified mermaid, whose head shot off in the direction of the chateau.

"AAARRGH!" screamed Nat, running for cover.

"BRILLIANT!" laughed Darius.

There was a final explosion of mermaid and water and feathers. Bits of cooked duck showered the garden. The lawn looked like it was covered in brown snow.

"NOOOO!" shouted the Baron, as he was hit on the head by a smoking beak. "Talk to me, Cecil, talk to me."

"Something smells nice," said Dad, emerging from the house.

He looked at the ruined garden, destroyed fountain, cooked fowl and murderously furious Baron.

"Oh dear," said Dad. "You don't know any good electricians, do you?"

CHAPTER TWENTY-SIX

••••

LATER THAT EVENING, DAD, NAT AND DARIUS WERE sitting miserably in a café in the village. No one had said much since the Baron had stomped off, threatening Dad with all sorts of dreadful revenge.

Nat had been especially quiet since the last of the unfortunate ducks had been shovelled into bin bags. She was beyond yelling. Even Dad must have realised that, in this horrible holiday, everything that *could possibly* have gone wrong had *actually* gone wrong.

(Obviously, THAT was wrong too; there were plenty more things to go wrong.)

A strange, weird calm had come over her; their fate was sealed – they would be a laughing stock, and there was nothing to be done.

She watched Dad toying with his plate of food. He looked glummer than she had ever seen him. She actually managed to try and cheer him up a bit.

"No one's ever tried to strangle you with duck gizzards before, Dad," she said, without emotion. "That's a first for you."

"I dunno," said Dad with a sigh, "just for once I'd like to do something properly."

"Be fair," said Darius, shovelling down a mouthful of food, "you properly exploded twenty priceless ducks in an electric fountain. That's real super-villain stuff, that is," said Darius.

"That's very kind of you," said Dad, a bit more cheerfully, "but I doubt the villagers will see it the same way."

Nat looked around the café, convinced the

locals would be sharpening their pitchforks and lighting their torches.

But she was WRONG.

When Dad tried to pay the bill, the café owner just said: "Zere is no charge for ze Great Slaughterer."

"The great *what*?" said Dad, who didn't like the sound of that one bit.

"Oh, just ze name you 'ave round 'ere," said the café owner, smiling.

Darius turned to Dad in awe. "The Great Slaughterer!" he said. "That's an AWESOME name."

Then the greengrocer came in with a bag of free spuds. Then the woman from the cake shop, with a free chocolate tart. The butcher gave them something squishy in a bag.

"I don't think the villagers like the Baron very much," said Dad, looking confused. Nat looked at Darius, who was sniggering.

"You should be a detective, Dad," said Nat flatly.

They found it hard to get away from the

café, as all the villagers wanted to meet the man who'd zapped the Baron's ducks. They were just making their way to the door when an old lady approached them. She was bent and wrinkly and warty and wore a big black shawl.

"She looks like the witch from *Hansel and Gretel*," Nat whispered to Darius. Even the Dog didn't want to go near her.

"He doesn't want to be a doggie doner," said Darius.

The old lady starting muttering at them, a stream of French that none of them understood. She clearly didn't speak English and Nat was relieved that at least Dad didn't embarrass her any more by trying out his Dad French. He looked quite nervous of her too.

The café owner translated. "Madame Morte, she is ze oldest lady in ze village. She knows all ze 'istory of everysink. She wants to know if you 'ave seen ze ghost yet?" he said.

And then he translated for them the creepiest story they had ever heard, told by an old, old lady in a creepy, crackly voice… The story of:

THE GREY LADY OF PETIT POIS.

Who haunted the attic of Posh Barry's house, seeking revenge for A GREAT WRONG that had been done to her.

Brilliant, thought Nat. *Just brilliant.*

In the van home, Nat was completely silent. Even by Dad's standards, this really had been a disastrous day. She hoped it wouldn't get any worse, shuddering as she remembered the ghost story.

Something tapped on the window and she shrieked in fright.

"What was that?" she said.

"Just a branch," said Dad.

"Warning us not to go any further," said Darius spookily. His face was deathly pale in the dim light of the van.

"Not funny, Bagley. None of this is funny. And nothing will ever be funny ever again. Is the electricity still off?" said Nat.

"'Fraid so," said Dad, "but I do have candles."

"How many?" asked Nat, praying he'd say a thousand.

"One each," he replied, as they pulled up outside the dark house.

"Isn't it funny how a house can look so nice in the daytime, but really ever so creepy at night?" said Dad as they opened the creaking front door and crept along the dark, silent hallway.

"Ever so hilarious, Dad," said Nat sarcastically. Her voice had a sinister echo. "But I'm not scared of gho—"

"Mwah ha HAAAA," said Dad very loudly behind her.

Nat screamed. Then she saw it was Dad. "Dad, what the HECK are you doing?"

"Lightening the mood," said Dad.

"What's that smell?" asked Nat, sniffing.

"Blood, probably," said Darius, "or ghost farts."

"It's white emulsion paint," said Dad. "Now stop it, the pair of you." He was starting to get spooked too. The house WAS very old and it WAS very dark. "We must stay together. Ghosts only show up when you're on your own. Everyone knows that."

"True," said Darius, blowing out his candle. "I'm going to catch it."

"Stop it, Darius," snapped Nat. "Darius?"

She looked round.

Darius was gone.

CHAPTER TWENTY-SEVEN

• • • •

THEY HUNTED HIGH AND LOW FOR DARIUS BUT HE was definitely NOT THERE. They started downstairs because downstairs was less spooky than upstairs. Their calls echoed around the dark, silent house. But all they heard were their own voices and their own footsteps, creaking on the floorboards.

"He'll be fine," said Dad. "He'll be watching us from somewhere, having a good laugh, the little... devil. We should ignore him; he'll come back."

"I know, Dad," said Nat, "but this house is dangerous."

"Come on, love, stop this ghost nonsense now," said Dad.

"No, I mean it's dangerous because you've been doing DIY in it," she said.

"Oh, I see. We should probably find Darius in that case," said Dad, now worried.

They braved the stairs and tiptoed along the dark passageway, listening to the rattling of loose window panes, and the drip of a tap and the thump thump thump of…

Thump thump thump?

"Aaarggh!" cried Nat. "Can you hear that thumping noise?" Then she immediately realised it was just her own heart beating and felt a bit daft.

Still scared, but daft as well.

They opened a bedroom door. Inside, the room was large and cluttered. There was stuff everywhere because the workmen had been using it to store all their tools and materials. There were boxes and paint tins, tools, ladders, pipes, bits of wood and metres of canvas cloth. Even in broad daylight you could have hidden a brass band in there.

"Bagley, you little monster, are you in here?" said Nat. "This isn't funny, you know. Come out so I can hit you."

"That's not going to get him to come out," said Dad. "I can see you don't know much about dealing with children. Where's his incentive?"

"I hadn't finished," said Nat. She addressed the room again. "But it won't be as hard as I'll hit you if you DON'T come out."

"Your mum's taught you pretty well," said Dad.

Still nothing.

They shut the door and tried the room at the very end of the corridor. "I haven't been in that room at all," said Dad. "It's been locked since we got here."

Nat tried the doorknob, expecting to find it locked as usual.

But it turned. It was *unlocked*.

Nat turned to Dad and caught her breath in fright.

A horrible face!

It was only Dad. He was holding the candle close under his chin and it made him look weird and quite scary. Nat swallowed hard.

Downstairs, the Dog suddenly began barking. "I'll see what that is," said Dad. "You wait here."

Dad walked quickly down the stairs… leaving Nat standing by the doorway. She told herself to stop being silly. She KNEW there was no such thing as ghosts. She also KNEW Darius was a little git.

She summoned up her courage and stepped inside the room. It was hard to see by the feeble candlelight, but it was clearly another bedroom. There was a huge old iron bed in the middle of the room and at first Nat thought it was another room being used as storage because there was something large dumped on the bed. But as she peered harder, she realised THERE WAS SOMETHING IN THE BED.

And that something was... ALIVE!

It was making strange snuffling noises, almost like someone snoring, but before Nat had time to wonder if ghosts snored, the light from her candle glinted off something terrifying.

There were teeth grinning at her from a bedside table! Two rows of sharp, white teeth, like from a skull!

And now something huge was rising from the bed. Something that was moaning and groaning horribly. And from out of the white sheets came a woman's grey face.

It was THE GREY LADY OF PETIT POIS!

An old, wrinkled hag of doom!

Nat thought her heart was going to beat right out of her chest and hop off down the stairs in sheer terror.

And then, horror piling upon horror, the ghastly thing *spoke*.

It said: "Is that you, Nathalia? I wondered when you'd turn up. Oh, your father's in for it, leaving me at the airport for two days. Hang on,

I'll just put my teeth in – I left them on the bedside table."

It was Nan.

CHAPTER TWENTY-EIGHT

• • • •

BAD NEWS NAN SAT IN THE CANDLELIT GLOOM OF THE kitchen. She was drinking tea and chomping biscuits and telling Dad off. Darius sat on her lap, sharing the biscuits. Darius had only recently reappeared, sulky he hadn't found an evil demonic spirit.

It was unusual for Darius to sit very close to anyone, because he didn't like it, and neither did anyone else. There were two exceptions: the Dog and Bad News Nan.

The Dog liked to sit near Darius because

Darius was always covered in stuff that humans classed as disgusting but dogs saw as tasty treats. Everything from baked-bean juice to bogies. It was always doggie feeding time with Darius. And Darius liked to sit near Nan and her biscuits for basically the same reason.

They were all now being forced to listen to an unbelievably long story about HOW NAN GOT THERE. Bad News Nan liked to stretch a story out. She called it 'filling in the details'. She could make a trip to the corner shop to buy a lottery ticket and a chocolate orange sound longer than Frodo's quest in *The Lord of the Rings*.

Nat said that to Dad once. He just grunted and replied that Nan would have done better than Frodo. He said: "If the Dark Lord Sauron had got wind of your nan coming to visit, he'd have chucked himself into Mount Doom from the start and saved all that bother."

After about an hour, Bad News Nan had still only got to the bit where she was at the airport back in England, having a row with the security people.

"They told me I had to take my shoes off to go through the scanner, but I said I'm not wearing shoes, am I? I'm wearing furry tartan slippers, because flying makes my feet swell up and if my corns burst there'll be hell to pay, young man. I said Elsie Dunlop at number seven, *her* corns burst and she never walked again. Mind, she had just dropped a microwave oven on them. I said to her, don't fetch those microwave ovens off the top shelf by yourself at your age with your pustulated discs, get an assistant, but she wouldn't listen. It was like when she tried to—"

"What happened at the airport?" interrupted Dad, eager to get to bed before dawn. They still had a house to finish.

"I'm *telling* you, Impatient Harry," said Bad News Nan. "I said, I am not trying to smuggle a nuclear warhead on to this plane in my slippers, I've never heard anything so ridiculous. They said if I carried on poking them with my umbrella they would arrest me, so I said why don't you arrest that man with a beard? He looks suspicious. Then they said he's an undercover policeman and by then I'd missed the plane."

Bad News Nan chomped the last biscuit but carried on talking, showering Darius with spitty crumbs.

Bad News Nan said she didn't know why Dad didn't know all this because she'd left loads of messages on his mobile phone.

Dad looked at the floor, deciding not to say anything about his phone getting cut off.

To cut a long story short, Bad News Nan had caught the next plane and then waited hours at the airport for Dad to come and pick her up, but Dad didn't show up. She had been talking to all the airport staff for ages and she said they must have really liked her because they all clubbed together to pay for a taxi so she could leave.

"But I couldn't believe what a horrible wreck this house was when I got here," she said, staring at Dad. "I said to the taxi driver, this can't be the right place. My son's working on this and I don't care what sort of a joke everyone back home says they're playing on him, he's NOT a – now, what was it they are all calling you?"

"Is it 'a really fun guy who's surprisingly practical and can turn his hand to anything'?" asked Dad hopefully.

"A monkey with a hammer," said Bad News Nan.

Hang on, thought Nat...

"What joke?" she asked. Dad looked worried; she had become as scarily quiet as Mum.

And then, Bad News Nan lived up to her name. She told them some really Bad News.

Posh Barry was telling everyone that he *never, ever expected Dad to be able to do up his wreck of a house*. He knew it was an impossible task. But he also knew Dad wouldn't be able to say no if Barry said it was for free. So he thought he'd let him have a go so they could turn up and see what a total mess he'd made of it – for a laugh.

"He said that as you think you're the funniest

man in town, you'd appreciate the comedy," said Nan.

Dad looked stunned.

Nat's voice grew even scarier, because it grew even quieter. It was almost a whisper now. "So, this whole thing... was a *practical joke*??"

But Nan wasn't done yet. She had one last punchline to deliver. "Oh yeah, and they're coming out a few days earlier too, to surprise you, because they thought it would be even funnier. They'll be here –" Nan looked at her watch – "day after tomorrow."

As final straws go, this was a barnful of hay, landing smack on top of Nathalia.

"Ah well," said Dad, smiling nervously at Nat, "it's pretty cruel but I suppose there's something a bit funny about it?"

Like the overheated engine on the Atomic Dustbin, Nat finally blew.

"Funny? *FUNNY*?? I've been chased, drowned, arrested, laughed at, pecked by birds, pelted with rotten fruit, haunted by ghosts, made to play with the most horrible kid in the world, *nearly electrocuted to death*, and it's supposed to be FUNNY????"

Dad looked thoroughly defeated. But Nat didn't stop there.

"We've got no time left to fix up this house before the Poshes arrive and make *even more* of a laughing stock of us than we already are, and even if we did have time, and this whole thing hadn't been a completely impossible job, and a total set-up by your *own stupid friends*, we would *never* have been able to do it *anyway*, because you can't even change a lightbulb or a fuse, let alone do up an entire house, because you are a complete PEANUT! And I'm not staying here to look like one too."

She stood up, knocking her chair to the floor.

"I want to go home. First thing in the morning. And I mean it, Dad."

She wasn't kidding.

Dad said nothing. There was nothing to say. He was beaten and everyone knew it.

Nat stormed out of the room and up the stairs. When she slammed her bedroom door, the whole rotten house shook.

It was over.

CHAPTER TWENTY-NINE

• • • •

Nat threw herself on the bed feeling about as low as she could ever remember feeling. It took her ages to get off to sleep, and when she did, she dreamed of Mimsy's pinched faced, laughing like a mad evil clown, and all her friends at school laughing along with her.

When she woke it was just before dawn, and she wasn't feeling any better. She started to pack her things, thrusting clothes furiously into her rucksack.

This holiday had been a total Dad disaster from

start to finish, thought Nat, and she just wanted to go HOME, to Mum, and Penny Posnitch, and *normal life.*

As she pulled out one of her school books from her bag, trying to fit the clothes in below it, a letter fluttered to the floor.

A letter addressed to her.

Confused, she ripped it open. As she read, her knees gave way and she sat heavily on the bed.

It was from Rocky.

It read:

Dear Nathalia,

I am sorry that our friendship has ended this way. With the sinkings and the explosions and the rotten vegetables and the police and everything.

Yes, it was a lively night, recalled Nat with a shudder.

But I am very fond of your father and I'll tell you why.

It is not because he's a good sailor. He's NOT a good sailor. He's a rotten sailor, anyone can see that. He should never be allowed near water again. I wouldn't let him within ten metres of a paddling pool, if I were you.

Yeah yeah, thought Nat miserably, *we all know Dad's rubbish. Big laugh, ha ha.*

But I like your father. and I'll tell you why. Because he is braver than me.

What? You must have brain damage from rotten tomatoes, thought Nat. *Have you seen my dad facing a spider?*

Just because I have sailed single-handed round Antarctica chased by killer whales. and skied down active volcanoes. and fought off crocodiles with my bare hands. doesn't mean I'm brave.

I have never been brave enough to be a father. I used to have a family back in England but I left to go and explore the world because I wanted adventure and I didn't want any ties. In looking after you the way he does. your father showed me true courage.

Being a good father is the bravest thing you can ever be.

Be kind to him.

Even though he is a massive idiot.

Love.

Rocky.

Nat read the letter a dozen times. By the last time, she'd come to a decision. She crept silently out of her room towards Darius's bedroom, tiptoeing so as not to wake Dad.

"Wake up, chimpy." Nat was standing over Darius, shaking him.

Darius opened one eye.

"Do you remember the way to the village?"

"Yes, now go away."

"Come on then, we need to go. NOW. Quickly, before Dad wakes up. Come on. I have a plan."

A few hours later, Dad was in the kitchen, frying bacon. "Hello, love," he said, looking up sadly as Nat came into the room. He had huge bags under his eyes, like he'd hardly slept. "I came to get you for breakfast but you weren't in your room," said Dad. "Where were you?"

"Outside," said Nat.

"Look, love, I'm sorry about everything. We're not too far from the airport," said Dad. "I'll drive you there after we've eaten. You and Nan can fly back, I'll bring Darius and the Dog home in the van. They can hide in the picnic basket again."

"I want to show you something," said Nat. "It's outside."

"If it's a bit of crispy duck I missed when I swept up, I don't need to see it," said Dad.

"It's not, I promise," said Nat.

They went outside. It was a beautiful morning. High clouds scudded over blue skies. It was like the world had been born again.

"Shame it's ended like this," said Dad with a sigh. "There were some less than terrible moments, I thought."

"Just watch the road," said Nat.

They stood there together for a few minutes. Suddenly they heard the sound of an approaching car. Or maybe a few cars. The sound grew louder. Dust from the road behind the hedge was billowing upwards. Cars were coming… lots of cars.

The first car to pull up was a bashed-up Land Rover, full of men from the village. They hopped out, brandishing tools. Then another car appeared and the same thing happened. Then a small pickup truck, loaded with pipes and bricks and wooden boards and paint cans.

"What's going on?" said Dad in amazement.

Nat slipped her hand into her dad's and gave it a quick squeeze. "We're in this together, Dad," she said, looking up at him. "You, me, and all the fans of the Great Slaughterer."

Dad looked like he might cry. *The soppy idiot*, thought Nat, kicking him.

"Let's get this house fixed up, shall we?" she said.

CHAPTER THIRTY

. . . .

THE MORNING WENT BY IN A BLUR. BY LUNCHTIME, the house was filled with the sounds of hammering, plastering, screwing, fixing and tea-making (the last one was Dad).

There were workmen EVERYWHERE.

There were THREE workmen ripping out the kitchen.

There were FOUR workmen and a digger churning up the garden.

There were FIVE on the roof.

There was a whole football team's worth

upstairs, redecorating.

The house was literally SWARMING with men. "Can you believe this, Dad?" said Nat when she eventually found him, calmly making yet another round of tea on a little gas stove in a workman's hut at the back of the house.

"Good, innit?" said Dad, munching on a chocolate biscuit and looking delighted. "I'm throwing them all a party tomorrow to say thank you."

"*What?*" said Nat. "A party?"

"It's called MOTIVATION" said Dad. "The more you give people, the more you get back. Look how many more people are helping out, now they know about the party."

Nat had to admit it was true. Another vanload of workers pulled up in the drive and men carrying wood and tiles and wires and bags of cement hopped out.

"But *tomorrow*? That's when Posh Barry and Even Posher Linda get here, remember?"

"That makes it even more perfect!" said Dad,

laughing. "It'll look like I've done it for them! Fixed the house AND organised a party. Not so useless, eh?"

Dad was really enjoying himself now. "Besides," said Dad, "not EVERY party I organise ends up in fires and explosions."

"Where shall we put the wood for the bonfire and these enormous fireworks?" asked a man holding a huge red box with pictures of fires and explosions on.

"Oh, drop them anywhere," said Dad lightly. Nat watched as logs and cases of high explosives were unloaded off a big lorry.

She was just working out what to be most worried about, when she noticed Gaston carrying a big plastic pipe nearby.

"What's HE doing here?" said Nat.

"He wanted to help," said Dad simply. "Said it's more fun than being at home."

"What's he doing?" asked Nat.

"Laying a new septic tank."

Nat gave up. She wandered off to find Darius,

thinking he was the most normal person she knew right now.

WHOA, your life has taken a wrong turn if Darius Bagley is the closest thing you have to normal... she thought to herself.

As if to prove the point, she almost tripped over Bad News Nan sunbathing on a lounger. She was sitting next to a huge pile of freshly dug earth, a digger and some scaffolding. It looked like she was relaxing on a bomb site.

"You OK there, Nan?" said Nat, shouting over the drilling and banging. A bit of earth from a trench flew over the mound and spattered into Nan's drink.

"Oh yes, love," said Bad News Nan, who was almost completely covered in towels and slathered in thick white cream to keep the evil sun at bay. She had such pale skin she reckoned she once got sunburned at night. She took her summer holidays in November and still came back peeling like a growing snake.

"This reminds me of the best holiday I ever had," she said.

Nat knew which that was. Last year Bad News Nan went on a bus trip advertised in the local paper, run by the man who usually delivered coal and shot weasels. It was ever so cheap because a) it was on a bus which smelled of coal and dead weasels and b) it was a trip to a resort the brochure described as:

Pre brand-new!

Which actually meant:

Not built yet!

Bad News Nan said it was brilliant because it was dead quiet, apart from all the concrete mixers and welding and jackhammers going off, but she preferred that to the horrible crowds and disco music you normally get on holiday.

She was lucky with the weather too; thanks to the howling winter gales the beaches were never crowded. Even the tourists who were not put off by the fish-processing plant down the coastline stayed away. They were all huddled indoors, or around the burning bins that kept the workmen warm.

As soon as Nan got back home she booked the same trip for next year.

Bad News Nan told Nat she still kept in touch with a welder called Plovdiv. *Yup*, Nat thought, *Darius is LITERALLY the most sane person I know. I'm so doomed.*

"BOO!" said a voice in her ear.

"Aaaarrgh!" she shouted, jumping. She turned round. It was Darius.

Then something screamed over her head with a great whoosh. Alarmed, she threw herself full-length on the muddy ground. A great bang went up nearby.

"Sorry, just testing a rocket," shouted Dad, who loved rockets. "No harm done, but watch out for sparks. That one's a lively one."

"Can you smell burning?" said Nat. She definitely could smell burning. There was smoke coming from somewhere…

It was coming from her! From the back of her jeans… A spark from the rocket must have fallen on them and now her backside was properly ON FIRE.

"AAAAARRGH!" she screamed.

"Jump in the septic tank," shouted Darius. "That'll put the fire out."

"Get lost," she shouted, running round in circles to try and get away from her smouldering bum.

At that moment, Dad saw Nat in trouble and quickly jumped up, dashed over and grabbed her, swinging her feet clean off the ground. He ran to a big plastic tub of water nearby and sat her in it, just as things were getting REALLY uncomfortable. *PSSSSHT!* went the steam. The workmen applauded.

"You have to be careful playing around here," said Dad, looking concerned, "it's quite dangerous if you haven't got your wits about you."

"Well, this is *humiliating*," Nat said as the workmen laughed and cheered at her soggy bottom.

"You do worry about what people think of you," said Dad.

Just then, someone grabbed his shoulder and spun him round. The Baron, with a look of evil triumph on his face, was standing in front on them. With a local policeman. Who looked a bit cross.

"Arrest them all," said the Baron.

"Hello," said Dad cheerfully. "Would you like a cup of tea? Kettle's just boiled."

"No zank you," said the policeman. "Ze

Baron 'ere says you 'ave ze little boy who 'as no passport."

Nat went cold.

"There's no little boy here," shouted Dad really loudly, walking around. "I BET YOU COULD SEARCH THE WHOLE GARDEN AND YOU'D NEVER FIND DARIUS BAGLEY. WHO'S VERY GOOD AT HIDING. NOT THAT THERE'S ANYONE CALLED DARIUS HERE."

"Why are you shouting?" asked the policeman. "I am one metre away. Zere is no need for ze shouting."

"Search everywhere, search NOW," ordered the Baron.

"Sterp ordering me about," said the peckish policeman, who was called Claude. "You are not ze Chief of Police. You are nurt even my wife."

Claude leaned in close to Dad's ear. "Since you massacre 'is ducks, 'e 'ates you very much. He may 'ave gone round ze corner."

"Bend," corrected Dad.

"Ah, zank you." Claude cast an eye over the garden. "Well, I can see no leettle boy 'ere, but I say to you now…" he spoke very loudly and clearly, "ze police are watching you. If we see zis boy and 'e 'as no passport, you will be in trouble, big time."

The Baron fumed, but copper Claude told him crossly that there was nothing they could do without *evidence*, and they left.

"We'll be back," said the Baron ominously. As he stormed off out of the garden, Nat noticed Gaston sloping out behind him. He caught her eye for a second, then looked away guiltily.

Why are you looking so guilty? Nat wondered.

CHAPTER THIRTY-ONE

••••

IT WAS WELL INTO THE NIGHT WHEN THE LAST OF the villagers downed tools and went home, promising to be back at first light.

There was only one day to go and the house was still half covered in scaffolding, but there had been an astonishing amount of work done.

The big hole in the roof had been patched up.

The leaks had been fixed.

Most of the lights worked.

The floorboards had been replaced.

The shutters had been mended.

The old paint and wallpaper had been sanded or ripped off, ready to be redecorated.

"The loo works!" shouted Darius, flushing like mad.

Even the mermaid in the fountain had her head back on.

The café owner was the last of the villagers to leave. Just before he got in his car he called Nat over, making sure no one else could see.

He handed her a note. "Ze little brat from ze chateau, 'e ask me to give you zis."

Nat eyed the note suspiciously, then went up to her room alone and opened it.

The note read:

Dear Mademoiselle Bumolé,

I have something VERY IMPORTANT to tell you.

I am not allowed to see you any more so please come to the chateau tonight when it is dark.

I will wait by an upstairs window round the back of the house.

Make the sound of a wild boar when you are there to get

my attention. There's lots of wild boars round here.

But be careful not to attract them with your wild boar impression. They bite.

Gaston.

P.S. I should probably tell you that my papa said if he ever saw any of you on his property he would shoot you with his big hunting gun and say he thought you were a burglar.

Thanks for telling me, thought Nat. *So that's boars and mad Barons I have to look out for. No thanks.*

I'm DEFINITELY not going now.

But after they all went to bed, her curiosity grew. What did he want to tell her?

I must be mad, she thought, getting dressed and putting her shoes on. She walked out of her bedroom, as quietly as a mouse. A little bit of her was excited. This felt like an adventure.

Then she trod on a ghost-trap and yelled in pain.

"Gotcha!" shouted Darius, leaping out of a cupboard. "Oh," he said, "it's just you."

"Get this off my foot and get lost," said Nat.

"Where are you going?" asked Darius.

"Nowhere. Don't follow me," said Nat.

She refused to tell him where she was going and made him promise not to follow. She didn't see he had his fingers crossed.

It was a cloudy night and very dark indeed. The chateau loomed large and rather monstrous as she approached. She crept round to the back of the big house and tried to see Gaston at a window. She had literally no idea what wild boars sounded like but guessed they were like a pig.

Feeling like an idiot, she started oinking.

"Zat is a pig, not a wild boar," said a voice high up at a dark window. "Eet is a rubbish impression."

"Gaston, you little monster," hissed Nat, "what do you want?"

But before he could answer, Nat heard footsteps from the side of the house, and saw the faint glow of a torch-beam.

It was the Baron!

"What do I do now?" said Nat, panicking.

"Climb up the drainpipe quickly," he said.

Nat was good at climbing but the drainpipe was old and rusty and it creaked alarmingly as she got higher. Nat thought for one horrible moment it was going to give way, but she managed to scramble to the top, just.

Gaston grabbed her and helped her in through the window just as the Baron passed by below. He shut the window behind her, drew a blind and put the light on.

Gaston's bedroom was like a very expensive toyshop: cars, remote-control choppers, robots, steam engines, boxes and boxes of action figures and piles of books and comics surrounded a huge bed.

Something pinned up on the wall caught her eye. It was a very pretty portrait of a young girl, in pastel and chalk.

It reminded her of someone.

Then she realised – it was a picture of her!

It was signed 'Gaston', along with the words: *Mon amie.*

Even Nat knew that meant: *my friend*.

That's me, she thought, *friend to local weirdos*.

This local weirdo was standing by the window, wringing his hands.

"What do you want to tell me?" she asked when she got her breath back.

It took him a while. He seemed nervous. "I wanted to say sorry." He took a deep breath. "It is my fault zat my father knows about Bagley. I told him."

Nat sat on the bed. Of course! That day at the chateau… she had told him. That was why he'd looked so guilty earlier.

"But why did you do that?" she said. And then Nat thought of the portrait of her. And she knew why.

Gaston was jealous.

Nat was furious, and felt sorry for him, and was a teeny bit flattered all at the same time. She wasn't used to being liked. *Can I help it that I'm so amazing?* she thought.

"Have you dragged me over here just to tell me

that?" she said sternly.

"I just wanted to say sorry. And to ask you please not to tell the Bagley. He will do 'orrible things to me in revenge."

Nat thought for a while. "He DOES like doing horrible things," she said, "and he does like revenge."

Gaston looked like he was going to be sick. "YOU told me about 'is passport," he said, "so it is your fault too."

"I know," said Nat, sighing. "Look, I won't tell him if you don't, OK?"

"OK!" said Gaston happily.

They shook hands on the deal.

"You know," said Nat, "we can ALL be friends. IF you play nicely…"

"I can do zat!" said Gaston, smiling. He opened the window. "Tomorrow I will come and 'elp with ze party. Be careful!"

Nat looked out of the window to the ground below. She could hear something moving in the bushes. *Probably just a mad wild boar*, she thought. *Great.*

Gaston could obviously hear it too. "Better go out ze back door," he said. "I'll show you ze way."

They crept through the dark house as quietly as they could. Nat wished Darius had shown her his ninja moves as he'd promised because their footsteps echoed loudly on the wooden staircase.

Finally they reached the bottom, and Gaston pointed to the back door, at the far end of the huge kitchen. Gaston started slinking back up the stairs nervously.

"I hear Papa," he said. "Ze key is in ze tray on ze shelf above ze door. Go, quick!" He crept back upstairs, and Nat ran for the back door.

She grabbed the door handle and tugged, just in case. It didn't budge.

She could hear footsteps.

Standing on tiptoes, she felt frantically around for the tray above the door but couldn't find one. At last, her hand settled on something cold and metal, but in her haste she knocked it off the shelf, and it landed on the tiled kitchen floor with a massive *CLANG* that echoed through the entire house.

Now she heard angry French words coming closer.

She was trapped!

The Baron's voice was getting louder. She couldn't understand what he was saying, but she reckoned the words *gun, hunting* and *burglars* were in there.

Suddenly she noticed the cat flap. It was quite big and she reckoned she could squeeze through. She dropped to her knees and put her head and shoulders through.

"Hello, Buttface," said Darius, who was standing on the other side of the door.

CHAPTER THIRTY-TWO

••••

66 **W**HAT ARE YOU DOING HERE?" SHE HISSED.

"Rescuing you," said Darius. "Say thank you."

"Just grab my arms and pull – I'm stuck!" Half of her was outside, but everything from the bum down was still in the kitchen. "How did you know I was here?"

"I followed you," he said simply.

"What on earth are you two doing?" said Dad, appearing behind Darius.

"Why did you tell Dad?" shouted Nat.

"He didn't – I followed him," said Dad. "What is *going on*?"

"What's going on is you're going to be stuffed and mounted over the fireplace, if you don't get me out in the next ten seconds," said Nat, trying to be quiet. "He shoots burglars."

"Get a move on then," said Dad.

"Thanks for the advice, Dad, but I'M STUCK, YOU MASSIVE IDIOT," she shouted, forgetting to keep quiet.

"Grab one of her hands and PULL!" Dad said to Darius.

They pulled.

"You're making it worse!" she said, feeling all the air squeeze out of her. She was jammed tight. She couldn't see what was going on behind her but she heard footsteps drawing closer. The Baron was right behind her. The back door swung open, Nat still wedged half in and half out of the cat flap.

"It's open," said the Baron.

"Evening!" said Dad to the Baron. "I'm definitely not a burglar."

"Zen what are you doing 'ere?" said the Baron. "And why is zis child in my cat flap?"

"Oh, THAT'S where she is," said Dad, playing for time. "She's, AH, she's, ER, she's, UM…"

"She's what?"

"SLEEPWALKING," said Dad. "That's it. She's a terrible sleepwalker. Don't wake her. In fact, best to go back to bed right now."

Dad put his hands under Nat and at last

managed to wriggle her free. He held her in his arms. She kept her eyes closed.

"Are you telling me she is currently asleep?" asked the Baron incredulously.

"Yes, ssssh," said Dad.

"I don't believe it."

"You can say what you want, she can't hear you," said Dad.

Oh no, thought Nat, *don't give him ideas.*

Too late. "Well, I'm sure you're telling the truth. I'll say goodnight."

Nat could feel Dad relax. *No, Dad, careful*, she thought, *he's up to something.*

He was. He said craftily, "Gaston tells me you are a very funny man."

Dad tried to look modest. "It's been said," he fibbed.

"I'm writing a speech for ze duck breeders' society tomorrow," lied the Baron, "but it's not funny enough. I wonder if you could tell me ze funniest joke you know?"

He eyed Nat's face carefully.

Don't do it, Dad, thought Nat. Because she knew that the more you are supposed NOT to laugh, the more likely you are to start giggling. And she was definitely not supposed to laugh.

But Dad couldn't resist.

Nat knew Dad thought that EVERY situation could be improved by making people laugh. Even when it was obvious that it sometimes made things far far worse.

"I heard a good one the other day," he began. Now, Nat NEVER thought Dad was funny, but right now…

SHE WASN'T SUPPOSED TO LAUGH.

Which suddenly made him – HILARIOUS.

She could already feel a little tickle start in her tummy. "There are two snowmen in a field," said Dad, "and one turns to the other and says: 'Can you smell carrots?'"

The Baron started to smile. Then he started to laugh. Then he started to roar, tears running down his face. "He he heeee," he gasped, "it is funny because their noses are MADE of carrots –

very very funny."

Then he stopped and stared at Nat. Fortunately she was still just about keeping a straight face. The Baron turned to Darius, who was skulking about next to Dad.

"Are *you* funny?" he asked.

Don't tell him, Dad, thought Nat. But of course, Dad did. "He does something very hilarious with his armpits," he said.

Oh no, thought Nat, *not fair*. Darius's armpit farts were officially the funniest thing in the universe ever.

"Let me see," said the Baron.

Darius, who had guessed the Baron's evil plan, just did a half-hearted one. It made a little farty noise.

Pfft, it went.

Nnnnng, went Nat inside. The little one was even funnier than the big one.

"One more time," said the Baron wickedly. "For me."

Darius tried to do an even quieter one but only

succeeded in creating a perfect one-cheek squeaker.

Ffffssssqrrrt, it went. Nat felt her whole body shake with suppressed laughter. *Make it stop*, she thought, *it sounds like someone trying to be sneaky and failing; oh that is hilarious.*

It was too much. She couldn't hold it in any longer.

"Ah ha ha haaaa," she laughed, jumping out of Dad's arms. "Hee hee hohooo ha ha. Oh, come on, I'm only HUMAN."

"I KNEW it!" shouted the Baron. "Burglars!"

Dad grabbed Nat's arm and they all ran like crazy and didn't stop until they were safely in their house, with the door bolted, and furniture piled up against it, just to be safe.

"Next year," said Nat, "we're going to Center Parcs like everybody else."

CHAPTER THIRTY-THREE

• • • •

NAT SLEPT VERY BADLY. MAYBE IT WAS HAVING NO window, maybe it was Bad News Nan snoring. Maybe it was the smell of fresh paint or the not-so-fresh septic tank. Maybe it was the thought of being chased by a gun-wielding baron.

Or maybe, she thought, tossing and turning, *it's knowing that tomorrow we'll be watched by police while trying to repair a WHOLE house, impress the Poshes AND put on a massive party.*

But however worried Nat had been, by late

323

afternoon the next day, several small miracles had happened.

Bad News Nan had stopped snoring.

The paint smell had completely covered the septic tank smell.

No one had been arrested or even lightly shot.

And most miraculous of all, by late afternoon Nat found herself standing outside a BEAUTIFUL OLD HOUSE.

It looked nothing like the old scary wreck it once was. The villagers sat on the warm grass, exhausted but happy.

Posh Barry and his rotten family would be arriving in just a few hours. In the nick of time, they had done it!

"It's amazing," said Nat.

"It's very nice," said Bad News Nan.

"Winner," said Dad.

"I preferred it haunted," said Darius from his hiding place in a bush.

"No more 'monkey with a hammer' jokes for me!" said Dad. "Told you I would get it fixed."

Everyone looked at him hard. All Dad had done was basically just make seven hundred cups of tea. "Yeah, well, someone had to *organise* everything," said Dad defensively.

"Can I stop hiding yet?" said the bush.

"No," said Nat, "just in case the police come looking for you. Now shut up and be more ninja."

"I'll miss the party. And I like parties."

Nat hadn't thought of that. She didn't know Darius liked parties. She didn't know he liked *anything* much except mayhem and destruction.

Oh, of course, she suddenly realised, *NOW I understand. Dad's parties ARE full of mayhem and destruction.*

"Why don't you hide with us?" said another voice, from another bush. It was Gaston. She had made Darius promise to be nice to him (in return for her promising to stop Bad News Nan from wiping his face with a spitty hanky every five minutes).

"Because I'm not being hunted by the cops, or *weird*," she said.

Gaston came out of the bush. He had twigs in his hair. "Darius is showing me his proper ninja hiding. Find me if you can!" he said excitedly, then ran off.

"You were gonna show ME your ninja hiding," said Nat, sounding a bit jealous.

"He's hiding from his dad so he can come to the party," said Darius. "And anyway, you told me to be nice to him."

Nat couldn't really complain. And besides, she wasn't in the mood to moan. She smiled, looking round at everything happily. The garden was now full of tables and chairs from local cafés. Someone had strung up bunting and fairy lights. There was a makeshift stage near the fountain of doom, now squirting water instead of lethal voltages.

Barrels of wine had been rolled in from somewhere. And there was a delicious smell of food cooking on a huge barbecue fire pit that the diggers had helpfully gouged out of the lawn.

Nat couldn't believe it. Despite all the disasters

on this trip, Dad had actually, somehow, DONE IT.

"I can't wait for the Poshes to get here," chuckled Dad, walking up and putting his arm round her. "They will not be expecting THIS."

Nat laughed. Dad was absolutely right. It was a pretty little palace; a holiday wonderland with lights and streamers and food and music and…

"…And when they come into the garden," said Dad, "it'll suddenly go *boom whizz bang*, as I let the fireworks off above their heads – *as if it's all for them* – and it'll be completely amazing and FOR ONCE Dad comes back a total hero."

Yeah, put THAT on your blog, MIMSY, thought Nat excitedly.

By eight o'clock, the Poshes still hadn't arrived but the party was well underway. Everyone was there except the Dog, who'd been exiled to a village house to keep him away from the fireworks, which he hated, and the roast chicken, which he loved.

All the village had turned up in their best clothes, ready to make merry.

Nat saw nice policeman Claude in charge of the barbecue. He was chucking great slabs of sizzling steaks and whole chickens over the bright glowing coals. Bad News Nan had volunteered to look after the cakes, which Dad said was a bit like letting Colonel Sanders look after a Kentucky henhouse.

The wine was pouring in the way it does when French people come anywhere near the stuff, and a little jazz band was on the stage, noodling away merrily.

So that's *jazz music, is it?* thought Nat. Not nice enough to actually listen to, but not so terrible as to get in the way.

Everything was perfect, really. Somehow, from the disasters of THE WORST HOLIDAY ANYONE'S EVER HAD EVER, Dad had finally, amazingly, got it right.

What a shame Darius has to hide in a cupboard somewhere, she thought, as she watched the barbecue smoke drift across the happy scene.

But then she realised it was very much for the best, and she hoped he was hiding safely, because someone had just arrived.

The Baron flipping Duckbrain.

And he'd brought with him a VERY UNINVITED GUEST.

SUSPICIOUS MICK!!!!!

Nat could not believe it. She almost fainted, like the heroines in OLD CLASSICS. Suddenly she understood why they swooned all the time. Suspicious Mick… *here*???

It was simply impossible.

But he was here, impossible or not.

He and the Baron were talking to Claude the policeman, who looked cross to be dragged away from his barbecue.

Nat ran over to Dad. He was opening bottles of wine and humming a happy tuneless Dad tune.

"Dad, *Dad*," she shouted. "Look who's here!"

"Suspicious Mick, I know," said Dad, who

didn't seem bothered. "He's a strange little man, isn't he?"

"But why – how – *what*?" said Nat.

Dad mixed some fruit into another jug of the local plonk. "Claude told me about him. Mick's one of those people who thinks that he's a real policeman just because he's got a uniform. No one likes them much, especially not *real* policemen."

Nat could see Claude arguing with Suspicious Mick.

"He's got one of those radios that listens in to the police," said Dad calmly. "He heard the rumour about a boy without a passport and volunteered to help find him. I reckon he's been following us for ages. Sad man. I'll just get him a drink."

Dad wandered off happily with two glasses in his hands. Nat felt sick. Darius was in real trouble and Dad was having far too much fun at his party to realise.

Nat felt so bad about dropping Darius in it that she had to confess what she'd done. She cornered

Bad News Nan over by *les gateaux*.

"And I didn't even know stupid Gaston liked me because he was always horrible to me," she said.

"That's how you can tell if a boy thinks you're really nice," said Bad News Nan, face full of cake. "Hasn't your dad taught you anything?"

Nat was about to reply when two soft hands went round her eyes. A lovely voice murmured behind her: "Guess who?"

It was MUM!

Nat sprang into her arms and wrapped herself tight. "Dad, Dad, *now* look who's here!"

"Hello, Ivor," said Mum as Dad wandered up, open-mouthed.

"How the—"

"Where's Darius?" said Mum loudly.

Nat froze. She pointed frantically to Claude, the policeman, who now seemed to be walking in their direction.

"WHO?" Nat said loudly. "WHO IS THIS DARIUS OF WHOM YOU SPEAK? I KNOW

NO ONE OF THAT NAME."

"Darius Bagley," said Mum. "I know he's here."

The Baron grabbed Claude, making him drop his sausage. He motioned to Suspicious Mick and the three of them approached Mum.

Nat's knees shook, but Mum did not seem concerned.

"Only I've got something for him," said Mum. And she held up a little battered book.

It was his PASSPORT.

"Now," said Mum, looking at Claude, Suspicious Mick and the Baron in turn, "is there anything else we can help you with, gentlemen?"

CHAPTER THIRTY-FOUR

••••

"How the...?" said Nat.

"But Oswald said..." said Dad.

As soon as the furious Baron had stormed off, both Nat and Dad turned to Mum in wonder.

"Yeah, Oswald might have been fibbing," said Mum. "After I got those jumbled messages on my answerphone, I decided I'd better try and track Oswald and the passport down. I'm good at finding morons in foreign countries."

Dad looked a bit uncomfortable. Nat giggled. Mum was totally awesome. She wondered if

Darius had been right after all. He was convinced Mum was a proper spy. She'd always laughed at this, but now she wasn't so sure.

"Oswald had taken the passport with him to Norway," said Mum. "I have a horrible feeling he was trying to sell it. I don't know if you know this but Oswald Bagley is not the nicest human being on the planet."

"No, he's not," said Dad. "I'm glad he's thousands of miles away. It makes me sleep more easily."

"Actually, he's here," said Mum. "I made a bit of a bargain with him."

"*What?* What *kind* of bargain?" said an alarmed Nat. "I read a play at school once about a man who made a bargain with the devil and that didn't go very well for him ONE LITTLE BIT, and that was only the devil, not Oswald flipping Bagley."

Just then a horrible throaty roar ripped the air and in a cloud of dust, a huge van appeared. On the side was painted:

My Filthy Granny

Four horrible-looking young men jumped off the bus, still wreathed in dust. They looked like ghouls.

Brave men from the village tried to hide their wives; less brave men hid behind theirs.

"They've had a terrible time, poor things," said Mum. "They've been banned from every country within five hundred miles of the Arctic Circle since Stinky Gibbon tried to bite the head off a penguin."

"They don't have penguins in the Arctic Circle, Mum," said Nat.

"They were at the zoo," said Mum.

"Ah, good old rock and roll," said Dad dreamily. "I should get my bongos from the van."

Nat cringed.

"I said that in return for Darius's passport," began Mum, "they would get—"

"Where's our free beer and food?" said Dirty McNasty, staggering over. "Only we ain't eaten since Oslo."

"Help yourself, boys," said Mum. Dirty

McNasty said, "Thanks," and gave Mum a shy smile. Nat was amazed.

"Feeding them was one part of the bargain..." Mum said.

"What time are we playing?" said Derek Vomit, in between great greedy mouthfuls of hot roast chicken.

"That was the other part," said Mum.

Stinky Gibbon was already stalking about on stage. The little jazz band dropped their instruments in terror and ran for it.

A huge black amplifier walked past.

"Hello, Oswald," said Dad. Oswald just grunted and carried on setting up the gear.

"Be nice, Oswald," said Mum sternly. Oswald grunted something again. "You have to be firm with him, that's all," said Mum.

"Your mum is officially more frightening than Oswald Bagley," murmured Dad.

Nat chuckled and stuck her tongue out at the Baron and Suspicious Mick and ran happily into the house shouting for Darius to tell him the good news.

After a few minutes of Nat shouting, Darius came trotting downstairs. Nat told him what Mum had done. He didn't seem surprised.

"I knew it would sort itself out," he said, "didn't you? You worry too much, that's your problem."

Nat froze. He sounded just like… Dad!

DARIUS BAGLEY WAS SLOWLY TURNING INTO DAD!

AAAARRGH! SHE WAS DOOMED, FOREVER.

"Where's Gaston?" asked Nat, recovering.

"Hiding somewhere," said Darius. "After four hours he gets his advanced ninja badge. Right, I'm off to get steak and chicken." He hurried downstairs, drooling.

Outside, Dad was shouting for her. "Quick," he said as she came out into the garden, "you won't want to miss this."

"Miss what?"

"The big moment. The Poshes," he said. "I've just seen their car. They're here!"

CHAPTER THIRTY-FIVE

····

DAD LOOKED LIKE A BIG DAFT KID ABOUT TO GET the world's biggest Christmas present. He pointed to a large sleek car pulling into the driveway. "That's Posh Barry."

Nat had to agree that this moment was PERFECT.

"Sorry about the joke, Captain Chaos," shouted Posh Barry, grinning out of the car window as he pulled up, not looking at the house yet. "Looks like you're still in one piece, at least."

"What are all these people doing on our lawn?"

shrieked Even Posher Linda from the passenger seat.

"OMG, *look*, Mummy," yelled Mimsy from the back seat, pointing at the house. "Look at our house…"

As the Poshes got out of the car, they stared at the beautiful, fairy-tale house, transfixed.

"LIGHTS!" shouted Dad, sounding smug. Someone threw a switch and a big floodlight lit up the restored house.

Posh Barry, Even Posher Linda and spoilt little Mimsy gawped, slack-jawed and open-eyed in wonder.

"FIREWORKS!" ordered Dad, even more smugly.

Fireworks lit up the clear night sky and the once neglected house sparkled in the light of a thousand new stars. Posh Barry looked at Dad in awe. Even Posher Linda wiped away a tear of joy.

"OMG times two," said Mimsy, "wait till I blog about my super brilliant new house!"

Go for it, thought Nat. *Blog away. My dad did that.*

A little later Nat stood in the middle of the party looking around in total amazement. Somehow the whole flipping trip had ended in triumph.

The band was rocking. (Mum said she had told them to play proper songs or they wouldn't get pudding.)

The fireworks were fab.

Darius was safe.

Bad News Nan was fast asleep face down in a chocolate surprise.

The Baron was staring at Darius and hopping up and down in frustration.

Claude was telling Suspicious Mick off, and every so often jabbing him with a fork. On the floor, in bits, lay Mick's police radio scanner, which Claude had jumped on.

Mum was cuddling Dad, which, OK, was gross, but they looked so happy Nat was prepared to overlook it.

It was amazing, brilliant, no – it was *perfect*. Just maybe everything she had ever thought about Dad was wrong.

"How does Dad always get away with it, Mum?" asked Nat.

"I have no idea," said Mum, looking affectionately at daft Dad doing daft-Dad dancing. "I think the world just LIKES an idiot."

Ten minutes later, Dad blew the house up.

CHAPTER THIRTY-SIX

••••

I T WAS THE POO THAT DID IT.

There are tons of things that explode: fireworks, dynamite, gas cookers, stage flares, petrol, dead whales on beaches, poo.

And ALL of these things (except for the whale) were at the party. All of them COULD have blown up the house, and in fact, they all did play a part in the disaster.

But it was the poo that did it.

Dad – smugger than ever before – had shouted: "ROCKETS!"

And the rockets had risen up into the night sky, filling it with sound and light and colour.

All except for the rocket that shot off sideways towards the house, disappearing into a big hole left by the diggers.

People clapped. Nothing went wrong. Nat was amazed. Dad was getting EVERYTHING right tonight.

And then…

There was a weird kind of loud thump underground, like when a really fat old lady sits on a fluffy cushion. A strange, thin blue flame began twisting ghost-like out of the ground in front of the house. A few people cheered, perhaps thinking it was part of the entertainment.

The plumbers who had worked on the house went pale. "Zat's gas," they yelled. "Methane gas – under ze 'ouse."

"EVERYONE RUN!" one of the workmen shouted. "BUT DO NOT PANIC!" added another, panicking.

As people started dashing about in confusion,

Dad asked one of the workmen what was going on.

"Somesink underground is alight," he said. "It might be ze gas from ze old septic tank. If zere's been enough poop over ze last two hundred years it could blow."

"Will there be enough?" asked Dad nervously.

Nat grabbed Dad by the arm urgently. "We're in France," she said. "Have you *seen* how much they eat over here? There'll be enough gas to blow the house into *orbit*."

"This is so cool," said Darius. "A poo-powered spaceship!" But then his face fell. "Oh," he said, looking worried.

This made Nat very worried indeed. Darius NEVER EVER LOOKED WORRIED.

"What?" asked Nat, dreading the answer.

"I locked Gaston in the attic," he said.

"Why did you do that?" shouted Nat, as the blue flame grew bigger. "Did you find out about me telling him about your passport and him dobbing you in to the police?"

"No, just cos he's annoying."

"Oh."

"But thanks for telling me you told on me though."

"Oh," said Nat again.

"I'll get you for that."

"Never mind me, what about Gaston? We have to get him out. Couldn't you have just given him like a big Chinese burn or something?"

"Already did," said Darius.

This was horrible. Over the noise of the party-goers they could hear the Baron calling for his son in the darkness.

Nat rushed over to Dad and gabbled out what had happened.

Then Dad did something amazing. His usual daft expression vanished and he *ran to the house*. It was too dangerous to go through the front door – blue flames were all around it.

"Claude," Dad shouted to the policeman, who was organising the mass exit. "Someone's trapped in the house. Get a ladder, now."

Dad meant business. Claude nodded, running

back with a massive steel ladder the workmen had left. He and Dad hauled it over under the attic window.

"Hurry, Ivor," said Mum anxiously.

"Hold the ladder tight," said Dad. Claude saluted. Dad climbed up the ladder quickly, and smashed his way into the attic window.

"Be careful, Dad!" shouted Nat.

Posh Barry and Even Posher Linda ran over. "What's that fool doing now?" said Even Posher Linda. Then more quietly, "I hope he's going to pay for that broken window."

"You've got five seconds to get out of my sight," growled Mum. Even Posher Linda backed away.

Mimsy held up her phone. "This is amazing," said Mimsy. "I'm going to film it all for my blog."

By now the Baron had joined the crowd.

"What is going on?" he said.

Someone shouted, "It's the Baron's boy. He's trapped in the house!"

"My boy…" said the Baron, immediately charging at the house and bursting through the crowd.

"Get back," shouted Claude from the house, but the Baron ignored him.

"That's my son up there!" he said.

Mum ran out and rugby-tackled the Baron to the ground. "It's too dangerous," she said, holding him down firmly. "Just wait here."

Darius looked at Nat, indicating Mum. "*Definitely* a secret agent," he whispered.

The Baron struggled. "He's all I've got," he said desperately. "Please save him!"

"Ivor will get him out, don't worry," said Mum. But Nat saw the worry on her face.

Nat stared at the house in fear. Blue flames flickered higher and higher, and awful cracking sounds came from under the house, but there was still no sign of Dad or Gaston.

Then, after an eternity of waiting, Nat saw a movement.

"He's coming out!" shouted Nat. And it was true. Dad was clambering out of the window and down the ladder, carrying the wriggling Gaston over his shoulder.

"Is he all right?" shouted the Baron. Mum released him and Dad dumped the boy on the grass at his feet.

"Thank you," said the Baron, who was pale with relief. He picked his son up. "My boy, are you OK?"

"I'm fine, Papa," said Gaston, smiling up at his dad.

Nat threw herself into Dad's arms. "That was the most stupid thing you've ever done," she said, pulling away and hitting him. Then she smiled and squeezed him tight again. "You're – you're amazing."

The Baron couldn't stop hugging his boy, and kissing the top of his head. Nat recognised the look on the boy's face – it was embarrassment! But she could tell he liked it too.

And then there was a horrible *CRUMP* from deep under the foundations of the house and everyone watched in horror as all the windows rattled and the walls shook and there was a terrible groaning and a fearful cracking…

…and the house *started sinking*.

"I did not see that coming," said Darius, impressed.

Down, down sank the house, straight down into the huge hole that was opening up beneath it.

"It must be a fault," said Mum.

"Yes," said Nat. "Dad's fault."

"No, I mean the explosion must have triggered a fault underground." Mum paused and thought a while. "But yes, it's obviously your dad's fault."

A huge cloud of dust and smoke poured from the yawning hole, making everyone cough and splutter. The smoke was lit by tongues of red and blue flame. It reminded Nat of the famous bargain with the devil.

"You might have been right about that deal with Oswald Bagley," said Mum, reading Nat's mind.

A minute later, it was all over. The house was gone, swallowed by the smoking earth.

Dad put a comforting arm round Posh Barry, who was too shocked to speak.

"You know how you said you wanted a swimming pool?" said Dad. "Well, you've got the hole."

THE BIT AFTER THE BOOK'S FINISHED

• • • •

I T WORKED OUT ALL RIGHT IN THE END. TURNS OUT THE world DOES love an idiot, after all.

Obviously there was a lot of shouting and wailing to get through first, but Nat was used to that; it wasn't unusual at the end of one of Dad's disasters.

The Baron offered to buy the land and the sunken house and turn it into a new duck pond and boating lake for Gaston. Barry and Linda quickly agreed, grabbed the cash, and Mimsy and went online to look for swanky modern flats near a beach somewhere.

The villagers all said it was the greatest party of all time and made Dad promise to do it again. Just not any time soon, please.

Gaston was happy to be alive and said thank you to Dad for saving him and thank you to Darius for locking him in the attic. After his rescue, he explained, his Papa was being very nice to him. He wrote Nat a letter to say thank you, and some others things, which Nat thought were VERY embarrassing, but she kept the letter anyway.

Mum was happy because it turned out she'd married a bit of a hero after all. His heroic rescue was even online – Mimsy posted the whole video on her blog.

Dad was happy that he'd proved he could fix a house without killing himself, like he promised.

"You're right, love," said Mum, "and you never promised you *wouldn't* reduce it to a buried, smoking pile of rubble after you fixed it."

Nat was happy that Dad was forced to promise

never EVER to pick up a tool again. "Stick to writing Christmas cracker jokes," said Mum. "They're not very good but at least no one gets blown up."

Darius was happy that he'd doubled his collection of rude words and could now be offensive in TWO languages.

Bad News Nan was grumpy at first because she'd slept through most of the action in some kind of chocolate pudding-induced coma. But that gave her something to moan about, so in the end even she was happy, on the whole.

Dad had even made Rocky happy. They got a note saying Rocky was going to find his family and say sorry for being such a rubbish dad – he said it was his "biggest challenge yet". Nat reckoned his biggest challenge would be stopping his kids thinking he was a total idiot, but agreed it was nice that he was making the effort.

The next day, Mum bought plane tickets back home for her, Nat, Darius and Nan.

"But the kids will want to come back with me in the Atomic Dustbin, surely?" Dad had argued. "We had fun getting here."

"You can have too MUCH fun, Dad," said Nat, with a smile.

At the airport, Dad kissed Nat and Mum goodbye. He ruffled Darius's hair and then quickly wiped his hand on the back of his trousers.

"Me and the Dog will be back home in a couple of days," he said, as they checked in. The Dog woofed in agreement.

"Yeah, right," said Nat to Mum, watching her daft dad waving them off, with a mixture of regret and relief. "I bet it takes him *weeks*."

She was right.

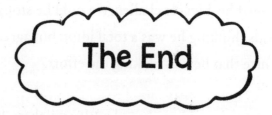

The End

More from

Nathalia BUTTFACE

Coming soon!

And here's a sneak preview...

"ARE YOU SURE NO ONE'S GOING TO SEE THIS video?" asked Penny Posnitch doubtfully.

"I'm not an idiot," said Nat, "I'm not my dad."

"Will you hurry up, my arms are getting tired," complained Darius.

"Just hold the camera straight and press the record button when I tell you," begged Nat.

The three of them were in her back garden. It was a lovely warm afternoon during the school holidays. The sun shone, the flowers were out,

Dad was upstairs trying to write Christmas cracker jokes and shouting rude words at his laptop and Nathalia and Penny were making a dance video.

The dance video was going very badly.

And so was Dad's joke writing. Every so often they would hear him yell: "Oh heck, that's not funny. I'm doomed!"

"I wonder if he needs a hand," said Darius, putting the camera down. "I've got a great joke about a monkey who needs to go to the toilet."

"The 'monkey who needs to go to the toilet' joke is not a joke anyone wants to hear while they're eating their Christmas pudding," said Nathalia. "Can we please do our dance video?"

"I want to hear the monkey joke," said Penny.

Nat started hopping up and down. "Aw, come on guys – I've been trying to make this video all morning, pleeease concentrate."

"I only came round to show Nat the new 'Dinky Blue, Girl Guru' episode online," grumbled Penny.

"She's rubbish," said Darius, making sick noises, "you should watch 'Doom Ninja Pete' instead. He blew up a pig last week."

"That's disgusting," said Penny, who was an animal lover.

Darius started doing his impression of a pig blowing up in slow motion, right up until the point when Nathalia ran over and started throttling him.

"Pick-up-the-camera-and-film-us-doing-the-dance..."

"OK," he squawked.

"Now, play the song on the phone."

"I can't remember the dance move after the song goes: 'Baby baby oooh baby'," said Penny.

"Which 'Baby baby ooh baby'?" said Nat. "She sings 'Baby baby oooh baby' about a ZILLION times. The song is CALLED 'Baby baby oooh baby'."

"Er – the first time," said Penny.

"That's the START of the song!" shouted Nat, in growing frustration. "I've showed you the moves about a thousand million billion times at least and I'm not even exaggerating. What is the matter with you? It's step left, arms cross, turn arms up, bend, slide and wiggle. Got it?"

"You're not a very good dance teacher," said Penny, "you're always shouting."

"That's how good dance teachers teach dance!" shouted Nat.

"Do you want me to film this bit?" said Darius, filming this bit.

"Of course I don't want you to film this bit. Stop filming this bit," said Nat, her long blonde hair flying out at all angles.

"When I saw Flora Marling's dance video there was no one shouting," said Penny, in a sulky tone.

"That's because Flora Marling is flipping perfect – we all know that," said Nat, "so this dance video has to be better than perfect."

"You can't be better than perfect," corrected Darius, who was filming with one hand while doing something disgusting with the other and his nose.

"I'm not doing anything while he's doing

THAT," said Penny, pulling a face.

Eventually, Nat got Penny to concentrate and Darius to wash his hands and after a few more shouty rehearsals, she and Penny were doing the dance.

Nat was especially proud of a new move she had invented called the Prancing Pony. It was super tricky and Penny had already got it wrong once and ended up in a hedge.

But finally it was going well.

"...up and hop and jump and slide and hop," whispered Nat, reminding Penny what to do, as they reached the tricky bit. "That's brilliant, Penny!" To her delight Penny was doing it BETTER THAN PERFECTLY when...

"I've gotta go," said Darius, putting the camera down on a hedge, "see you."

"WHAT? We haven't finished, you total chimp," said Nat.

"Then you shouldn't have taken so long," said Darius, walking off through the back gate, "I'm busy."

"Doing what? Where are you going?" Nat shouted after him, but he was gone.

"Just thought I'd see if you two were OK," said Dad, appearing from a bush, "I was watching you jiggle about and it looked like you'd swallowed space hoppers."

"THAT'S IT!" yelled Nat, throwing herself on the grass. "I can't work like this."

"Ooh, you taking selfies?" said Dad, picking up the camera. "Urgh, why's this camera all sticky?"

"We are NOT taking selfies," said Nat, "and I don't even know why you know about selfies – you're too old."

"What are you up to then?" said Dad, adding jokingly, "I hope you're not thinking of putting anything onto the online inter cyber-space web."

Nat hadn't been intending to put her dance video online but she didn't want to be told she COULDN'T.

"Can if I want," she said. She wasn't usually this rude but she was hot and tired and frustrated and scratchy.

"Stop showing off in front of your friend," said Dad, gently, which was one of the MOST ANNOYING THINGS HE COULD SAY. It was up there with:

You're only grumpy because you're tired.

You're only grumpy because you're hungry.

You're only grumpy because you've found Nan's false teeth in the biscuit tin again. AFTER you've eaten a Digestive.

"I am NOT showing off, Baldy," said Nat, showing off. "And this dance routine could get me a million hits and make us lots of money and then you'll be sorry."

"You're very grumpy," said Dad. "You must be tired. Or possibly hungry. Or have you been in the biscuit tin?"

"You said you wouldn't show anyone this video," hissed Penny. "You promised."

"Why is everyone always telling me what to do?" said Nat.

"Online is a very dangerous place," said Dad, patiently. "Do you remember when you and

Daddy had that talk and Daddy said it was like a big nasty dark cave with monsters in it and you said it sounded very scary and you promised to stay outside the cave forever and ever?"

"Yes, when I was SIX, Dad," said Nat. Penny sniggered. Nat felt herself getting red in the face.

"Every flipping day!" she yelled, waving her arms about like mad, "you always embarrass me. People are watching, Dad, can't you be NORMAL?"

With that she ran out of the garden.

And into... fame.

CHAPTER TWO

• • • •

NAT DIDN'T GET FAMOUS IMMEDIATELY; IT TOOK HER the whole weekend.

And of course it took the power of what Dad annoyingly always called the 'online inter cyber-space web' to make her famous.

Nat was blissfully unaware of the fuss she was causing online because, for a start, she had no idea she WAS online...

Plus, the next couple of days she was totally OFFLINE. Mum came home after having been abroad for two weeks, with her new job, and Nat had *loads* of catching up to do. She never even noticed when the battery on her mobile phone ran out.

And so she missed A LOT of texts from her friends...

Texts like:

OMG!!! LOL. ROFL.

And

YOU ARE SOOOOO FUNNY.

And

HAVE YOU SEEN YOURSELF??????

And

U R A ✳

Most of the catching up with Mum was spent clothes shopping while telling Mum how utterly rubbish Dad had been recently.

The Atomic Dustbin – Dad's horrible old camper van – had broken down twice picking her up from school and once when he'd volunteered to take the hockey team to an away match.

"We were so late the other team were allowed to start without us and we were 10–0 down before we even got on the pitch," she complained, making Mum giggle.

Then she revealed Dad had made them pork pie and chips for tea THREE times last week. And it would have been four times but Bad News Nan came round and insisted they have a proper meal with vitamins and then ordered pizzas because cheese counted as veg, near enough.

Mum's shoulders shook as they picked out tops.

"He does look after you pretty well, though," chuckled Mum, in the changing rooms. "I mean, compared to being looked after by a trained gorilla."

"Why are those girls staring at me?" said Nat, noticing a gaggle of gigglers, pointing and sniggering in the shop doorway. "Are my pants showing?"

Mum came out of the changing room and raised her eyebrows at the girls, who took the hint and ran off. Nat LOVED the way Mum could do that. She had seen Mum reduce grown men to quivering jelly by the simple raising of her fearsome eyebrows. Even the policemen who were always telling her off for driving much too fast in her little red car.

Dad couldn't scare anybody, thought Nat. *He only makes people laugh, the big dope. Even when he's TRYING to be fearsome.*

Nat sometimes practised raising her eyebrows at Darius when he was being especially annoying, but he just laughed and said it made her look cross-eyed.

"Can't you be NORMAL?" shouted one of the girls outside, and the others shrieked with laughter as they took off through the shopping centre.

What a weird bunch of girls, thought Nat. Within five seconds she forgot all about them because Mum said she'd buy her a new pair of flip-flops.

But a similar strange thing happened as they were choosing a DVD to play that night. Nat was having a good-natured argument with Mum as they wrangled over a big disaster movie (Mum's choice) or a film about girls who win a singing competition and sing a lot (Nat's choice). Dad wasn't there; he was just going to have to watch what he was told.

Nat couldn't figure out how she knew, but she suddenly became aware of a couple of boys over by the comic book films who were sniggering and looking over at her. She glared at them and they slunk off.

"People are watching," one said, for no apparent reason.

But, yet again, Nat soon forgot all about it because she heard Mum say she was going to the bath bomb shop next.

It was only late on Sunday night, in bed, snuggled in and smelling of crème brulee bath bomb that Nat plugged her phone in and was instantly greeted by a million bongs that told her SHE HAD MESSAGES.

So finally, she read them...

Have you read?